'A marriage?' Incredulity didn't cover it—this was stark disbelief! **'We get married so you can share a tent with me? In an earthquake-stricken village where the choice of shelter is non-existent?'**

'It is an old arrangement—usually made for the convenience of both parties, but without the obligations of a real marriage. It is legal to do this, to make a *misyar* marriage for our convenience so the people do not think that I am shaming you, nor that you are a shameless—'

'Hussy is the word we'd use,' Alex said, actually chuckling as she said it. 'I can't believe this. It is just too weird. I know other cultures have their boundaries, and it's the difference between people that makes the world the fascinating place it is, but—'

Laughter swallowed up the words, and now instead of fanciful smiles in the night air Azzam felt the stir of anger.

'Is marrying me so ridiculous?' he demanded. 'Many women would be gratified to—'

'Be proposed to by a prince?'

Dear Reader

From an early age I have been fascinated by the folk tales and fairy stories of the Arab world. *The Seven Voyages of Sinbad the Sailor, Ali Baba and the Forty Thieves, Aladdin's Wonderful Lamp*—all the stories Scheherazade spun to the Sultan to save her life—were part of my childhood, and the illustrations, the images they evoked, have remained with me all my life. So writing sheikh stories seemed a natural extension of this childhood fascination. Having visited many of these areas, experienced the fascination of the markets, seen lamps just like Aladdin's, and touched the huge jars the forty thieves might have hidden in, my interest has become greater—which is why a sheikh story seems to bob into my head at least once a year.

This story was special, because I leave the intrigue and mystery of the cities behind and spend most of the book in a small remote village, devastated by an earthquake. Out of the devastation a special kind of love takes seed, grows, and finally blooms.

Meredith Webber

SHEIKH, CHILDREN'S DOCTOR... HUSBAND

BY
MEREDITH WEBBER

First published in Great Britain 2011
by Mills & Boon,
an imprint of Harlequin (UK) Limited,
Large Print edition 2011
Eton House, 18-24 Paradise Road,
Richmond, Surrey TW9 1SR

© Meredith Webber 2011

ISBN: 978 0 263 21746 9

Harlequin (UK) policy is to use papers that are
natural, renewable and recyclable products and made
from wood grown in sustainable forests. The logging
and manufacturing process conform to the legal
environmental regulations of the country of origin.

Printed and bound in Great Britain
by CPI Antony Rowe, Chippenham, Wiltshire

Meredith Webber says of herself, 'Some years ago, I read an article which suggested that Mills and Boon were looking for new Medical™ Romance authors. I had one of those "I can do that" moments, and gave it a try. What began as a challenge has become an obsession—though I do temper the "butt on seat" career of writing with dirty but healthy outdoor pursuits, fossicking through the Australian Outback in search of gold or opals. Having had some success in all of these endeavours, I now consider I've found the perfect lifestyle.'

Recent titles by the same author include:

BACHELOR ON THE BABY WARD*
FAIRYTALE ON THE CHILDREN'S WARD*
DESERT KING, DOCTOR DADDY

Christmas at Jimmie's collection

CHAPTER ONE

HE'D send for her!

No, he'd go himself.

Shouldn't there be someone else to handle things like this? Monarchs of their country shouldn't have to check out women who'd intruded themselves into the royal family.

His father certainly hadn't checked out Clarice.

Perhaps if he had, things would have been different…

His Supreme Highness Sheikh Azzam Ghalid bin Sadiq, newly anointed ruler of Al Janeen, groaned and buried his head in his hands as the random thoughts whirled around inside his head.

As if his father could have done anything to prevent his twin brother's marriage. Bahir had fallen in love with Clarice the moment he'd laid eyes on her, not noticing that Azzam had already lost his heart to the beautiful woman. But it was the way Clarice had transferred her attention from him to Bahir that had staggered Azzam, and her behaviour since, the pain she'd caused his brother, had left Azzam with a deep distrust of women.

That is a ridiculous bias, the sensible part of his brain told him. You're judging all such women by one example—totally unacceptable!

Yet deep inside he knew the hurt had never really healed—Clarice's betrayal had cut deep, leading to him shunning most female company over the last few years and seeking solace in his work.

Which didn't solve the problem of the stranger in their midst!

He'd see her himself. *He'd* handle it.

He left his office, his mind churning as he entered the wide colonnade surrounding the courtyard gardens, striding towards his mother's favourite sitting area.

Striding—but reluctantly.

He'd met his mother off the plane on her return to Al Janeen, but in the cluster of chattering women disembarking with his mother he hadn't noticed a stranger among them.

Had she deliberately hidden herself among the other women?

He tried to ignore the alarm bells ringing in his head but the parallels with Clarice's arrival in his country were just too strong to be ignored. Back then, it had been him, not his mother, Clarice had accompanied, him she'd fussed over on the flight, convincing him he'd need a massage therapist once the cast was off the leg he'd broken in a skiing accident.

Not that he'd needed much persuasion. He'd been attracted to the golden beauty from the first moment he'd set eyes on her, fallen in love with her within days, only to find that once she'd met Bahir and realised *he* was the heir, Azzam had been dropped like a smouldering coal.

Azzam couldn't say for certain his sister-in-law was responsible for his brother's death, although he knew her continual and extravagant demands had weighed his brother down. Then there was the talk of fights and arguments that was surfacing among the staff—one story in particular of a loud and bitter altercation before Bahir had driven off in his car that fatal day...

It could all be rumour-mongering, but Azzam had to admit that recently Bahir had been patently unhappy, though he, Azzam, had been too busy with his own interests—with his passion for the new children's hospital—to seek too closely into the cause.

The pain this knowledge caused outweighed all other—to have failed his brother, his twin, his other half! Although, could he have done anything? Interfered in his brother's marriage?

Azzam knew he had to stop groaning. Groaning achieved nothing. In fact, it was weak and wimpish—he was behaving like a fool!

He had to pull himself together and behave like the ruler of the country.

He had to check out this woman, for a start. His mother was particularly vulnerable at the moment, and he didn't want anyone taking advantage of her then upsetting her further by letting her down. That, too, had happened in the past...

Straightening his shoulders, he strode on towards the shaded area where his mother sat each afternoon with her friends and female relations.

What was she doing here?

How *had* she let herself be persuaded to fly off at a moment's notice to some foreign country?

What about her *jobs*?

The hospital had assured her, when Alex had phoned them, that they would always have her back. Doctors willing to work nights in emergency rooms were always welcome. But how long would the clinic keep her second job open? She'd thought maybe they'd pay her while she was away, as technically Samarah was their patient, but that idea had been slapped down, the manager telling her if she took time off to accompany Samarah back to her home, it would be without pay.

Pay she desperately needed. But when Samarah had wanted her help, she hadn't had the heart to refuse.

Alex pondered the situation for the hundredth time as she lay back on the silk-quilted bed. No answers were forthcoming so she looked around the sumptuous surroundings, trying to take it all in so she'd remember this part of the dream in which she found herself.

She was in a room with dark red walls, hung with what looked like very fine carpets—tapestries perhaps—woven into fascinating patterns with jewel colours of emerald, ruby and sapphire, and the shadows on the silk coverlet on which she lay were formed by fretwork across open windows, what looked like marble carved into patterns as intricate as those in the carpets on the wall. More carpets were layered on the floor, so when she stepped off the bed her feet sank into softness. Above her, silk sheets like those on which she lay were draped from a central point in the ceiling so she had the impression of being in an extremely luxurious tent.

Her journey had taken on the aspects of a magic-carpet ride to a fabled world, for here and there around the rooms were huge brass urns like the ones in Ali Baba's story, and strange-looking lamps Aladdin would have recognised!

It's an adventure, she told herself.

Enjoy it.

Work will wait.

Oh, how she longed to believe that—to relax and enjoy the thrill of the new—to see something of the world beyond this room, the wide, empty desert, the rising red dunes, the colour and scents of the markets and the noisy delight of the camel auctions Samarah had spoken of with such vivid words and obvious love.

Impossible, of course, Alex knew that much! The reason she worked two jobs wouldn't wait—not for long. Bad enough that her brother had cheated his bosses, but how could he have been so stupid as to get involved with dodgy money-lenders? With people who would have no qualms about threatening his wife and vulnerable daughter?

Alex sighed, then turned her attention to practical matters, like getting out of this country she was yet to see.

Apparently Samarah had a niece who was a doctor. As soon as she returned from overseas, Alex would be free to leave. Samarah's son, the king, was also a doctor, but Samarah was adamant it was not his highness's job to look after her.

In the meantime?

For a start, she should get up off the bed, find her way outside, possibly dropping breadcrumbs on the way so she could find her way back, and have a look around. Arriving in the dark of very early morning, she'd gained nothing more than the impression of an enormous building, more like a walled town than a house. She'd been led along dimly lit corridors, past shadowy rooms, then seen Samarah settled into bed, sat with her a while until she slept easily, then slept herself. Now daylight was nearly done and she'd seen nothing—

'Please, you will come.'

The young woman who'd been fussing over Alex since she'd woken up halfway through the afternoon was hovering in the doorway.

'Samarah? She's sick again?'

Alex shot off the bed as she asked the question, looked around for her shoes then remembered she'd left them in the doorway the previous night. She brushed back the stray hairs that had escaped her plait, and followed her guide.

'Samarah is there but it is the prince who wishes to see you.'

'The prince?'

'His new Highness.'

It was all too confusing, so Alex kept walking, trusting that a conversation with this august personage would sort out a lot of things, not least of which was when she could return home.

Her carer led her out of the building, into a covered colonnade that joined all the houses around a beautiful central courtyard, with fancifully shaped trees, and massed roses in full bloom and fountains playing tinkling music, the cascading water catching the sunlight in a shimmer of such brilliance Alex felt her breath catch in her throat.

What a beautiful, magical place...

'Come, come,' the woman urged, slipping on her sandals and motioning for Alex to do the same, but although Alex responded, she did so automatically, her mind still lost in the delight of her surroundings.

That all this lush beauty should be hidden behind the high walls she'd glimpsed last night!

They walked around the colonnade, passing another dwelling, eventually reaching the end of the rectangular courtyard. In front of her, Alex could see carpets spread, with fat cushions and a low settee placed on them. Samarah was there, and some of the women who had been in Australia with her, their low-voiced chatter reaching out to Alex, making her feel less apprehensive about this meeting with the 'new highness'.

But as she drew near, the women moved away, drifting lightly down into the courtyard, Samarah among them, so only a man in a white robe remained on the plush red velvet settee on the vivid carpets.

Azzam looked at the pale, tired woman who appeared in front of him. Not a golden blonde, more a silver ghost, slim and insubstantial, the shadows beneath her grey eyes the only colour in her face.

Was it the strain he read on her neat features—a strain he knew was visible in his own face—that made him pause before he spoke? Or did he have some fundamental weakness—some predilection for blondes—that clouded his judgement?

That suspicion, though he instantly denied it, strengthened his will.

'I am Azzam,' he said, standing up and holding out his hand. 'My mother tells me you have been good to her and I wish to thank you.'

'Alexandra Conroy,' she replied, her voice soft but firm, her handshake equally solid. 'And I've done no more for your mother than any doctor would have done. Adult onset asthma is not only very distressing for the patient, it can be extremely serious.'

She paused and the grey eyes, made paler by their frame of dark lashes, studied his face for a moment before she added, 'But of course you'd know that. You're the doctor, your brother was the lawyer.'

Another pause and he saw her chest rise as she drew in a deep breath.

'I am sorry for your loss. It is hard to lose a sibling, doubly hard, I would imagine, to lose a twin.'

The simple, quietly spoken words pierced his soul, the pain of losing Bahir so acute that for a moment he couldn't speak.

Had it been the wrong thing to say? Alex wondered. She found the man's silence discomforting, but more distracting was the glimpse she'd had of his eyes—a startling green, gleaming out of his olive-skinned face like emeralds set in old parchment.

'Please, sit,' he eventually said, his voice cooler than the evening air, making Alex certain she'd breached some kind of protocol in mentioning his brother's death. She eyed the cushions, then the settee, which had taken on the appearance of a throne as she'd approached. But he waved his hand towards it, so she sat, then regretted it when he remained standing, putting her at an immediate disadvantage.

'My mother's asthma? It came on suddenly?'

If a discussion of his mother's health was all he wanted of her, why was she feeling uneasy?

Because there's an undertone in his voice that sounded like—surely not suspicion...

She was imagining things.

Yet the sense that this man was judging her in some way persisted, making her feel uncomfortable, so her reply was strained-hurried.

'I work for a clinic that does—I suppose you'd say house calls—to hotels on the tourist strip of the Gold Coast. About four weeks ago, the clinic had a call from the hotel where your mother was staying. I was on duty and I found her breathless and fatigued, and very upset, which wasn't so surprising as it was her first such attack.'

'You treated her?'

An obvious question, yet again she heard some underlying emotion in it.

Putting her silly fancies down to tiredness, not to mention an inbuilt distrust of men as handsome as this one, she explained as concisely as she could.

'I started with an inhalation of salbutamol, then a corticosteroid injection. Her breathing became easier almost immediately, but I put her on oxygen anyway, and stayed with her. The next day, when she was rested, I talked to her about preventative measures she could take to prevent another attack. I explained about having a management plan for the condition.'

'I can imagine how well she took that,' the man said, and Alex thought she caught the suggestion of a smile lifting one corner of his lips. Unfortunately, it drew attention to his lips, so well shaped an artist might have drawn them. Something that *wasn't* apprehension fluttered inside her. 'Not one to take even a mild painkiller for a headache, my mother.'

Alex nodded, and forgot her suspicions, *and* the flutter, enough to smile herself, remembering the battle she'd been waging with Samarah to convince her that prevention was better than suffering the attacks.

'You're right, although after the second attack I think I was gaining some ground.'

Her smile changed her face, Azzam realised. It lifted the tiredness and smoothed out the lines that creased her brow, making her not exactly pretty but—

She was speaking again. He had to concentrate.

'Unfortunately, when the news of her son's death came, it triggered the worst attack. She was desperate to return home, but I couldn't in all conscience let her travel without medical care. A competent nurse could have handled it, but

Samarah had come to know me as I'd called in most days over the weeks since I first saw her. I suppose she felt safer with me beside her, so I flew here with her and her friends. As you know, we broke the journey in Singapore, stopping over for the night so she could rest.'

'And now?'

Azzam knew he'd spoken too abruptly, his voice too cold, too remote, but once again the past seemed to be colliding with the present— Clarice's insistence she fly to Al Janeen with him—this woman coming with his mother.

The woman's smile gave way to a frown as she re-sponded.

'February is our most humid month at home. Although your mother was in a hotel, she'd had the air-conditioning turned off in her suite and she insisted on walking on the beach beside the surf every day. I am assuming it was the humidity that triggered the attacks and now she's back in the dry air here, she should be all right, although with adult onset, the asthma could persist, and she did have a mild attack on the first stage of the flight.'

Again Alex paused. A woman who thought before she spoke...

'I believe she has a niece who is a doctor and who normally takes care of her health, but apparently she is away.'

Was she angling to stay on?

His mother would like her to—he already knew that—but previous experience suggested the sooner the stranger was gone the better. His mother would settle down with her friends, he'd get on with the mammoth task of learning his new role, and everyone would be happy.

No, happy was definitely the wrong word, but life could begin to return to normal—a new normal, but still...

'So?'

The word came out like a demand, unintended, but she was disturbing him in ways he couldn't understand. So quiet, so shadowy.

Insidious?

But if his mother needed someone to keep an eye on her, which she obviously did, then this woman...

'I suppose it's up to you,' she said. 'But I won't

leave Samarah without competent care. Is there someone else who could keep an eye on her until her niece returns?'

Alex wanted to suggest he do it himself, despite Samarah's protestations, but there was something forbidding in the stern features of this man.

And what features! They drew her mesmerised gaze as a magnet drew iron filings—the high sculpted cheekbones, the deep-set eyes, the slightly hooked nose—a face that looked as if the desert winds she'd heard of had scoured it clean so the bones stood out in stark relief.

Hard as weathered rock…

She was still cataloguing his features when he replied so she missed the early part of his sentence.

'I'm sorry?' She was so embarrassed by her distraction the words stumbled out and seemed to drop like stones onto the carpet where Azzam was pacing.

'I asked if you feel my mother should stay on preventative medication now she has returned home.'

Was it suspicion she could hear in his voice? Was *that* the note bothering her?

Or was it pain? He'd lost his brother, his twin—his world had been turned upside down...

Realising she should be speaking, not thinking, and relieved to have an easy question to answer, Alex now hurried her reply.

'Probably not in the long term, but for a while perhaps it would be best if she continued to take leukotriene modifiers. I've been monitoring her lung capacity with a peak-flow meter daily and prescribing preventative medication as needed, but she is reluctant to use the meter herself and to take control of the illness.'

To her astonishment, the man smiled. Smiled properly, not just a lip quirk. And it was a smile worth waiting for, because it lip up his stern face the way sunrise lit the highest peaks of a cold mountain.

Alex gave a little shake of her head, unable to believe the way her mind—not to mention the fluttering thing inside her chest—had reacted! Sunrise on a mountain indeed! She was losing it!

Tiredness, that was all!

She looked at a point a little above his right shoulder so she didn't have to see his face again, and concentrated on his words.

'You are asking her to do something against what, she believes, is meant to be. She would see, and accept, her illness as the will of God. Can you understand that?'

Alex nodded, then, for all her determination not to even look at him, she found herself returning his smile as understanding of Samarah's opposition became clear.

'Ah,' she said. 'I did wonder why she was so adamant about it, but if she feels that way, of course she doesn't want to interfere in what she feels should be beyond her control. Can *you* persuade her? Could *you* convince her that she is better off taking mild medication than having to take the really heavy-duty stuff when she has an attack?'

His smile had slipped away, and he looked darkly grave, as if, in his mind, *he'd* slipped away, and to a not-very-happy place.

'My brother could have,' he said quietly, and this

time she heard the pain distinctly. 'My brother could have charmed the birds from the trees so my mother was easy work for him.'

He paused, looking out over the delights of the garden courtyard, and Alex imagined she could feel his pain, throbbing in the air between them.

'I will try,' he said, 'and in the meantime you will stay, care for her, until Maya, her niece, returns?'

Although the invitation sounded forced, as if the man felt he had no alternative but to ask, Alex's immediate reaction was to agree, for she'd grown very fond of Samarah and certainly wouldn't leave her without competent medical support, particularly while she was grieving for her son. But money, something Alex had never thought she'd have to worry about, reared its ugly avaricious head, and she hesitated.

As the full extent of Rob's indebtedness had became obvious, she'd promised her dying mother she'd repay his debts, clearing the family's name and restoring its honour, but beyond that promise was the fact that her sister-in-law, unable to work herself because of her daughter's special needs, was relying on her. No way could Alex let these much-loved people down.

An image of the money-lender's henchman rose up in her mind, clashing with memories of the promise. She'd met him only once and that had been enough. There was no way she could allow that man to terrorise her sister-in-law or her frail little niece.

Alex drew in a deep breath. It was useless. No breath could be deep enough for what she was about to ask, so she blurted out the words she hated having to say.

'I can stay. I'd be happy to, but personal reasons mean that I can't stay unless—'

She balked! She couldn't do it!

'Unless?' he prompted, and she knew the coldness and suspicion she'd imagined she'd heard earlier had returned to his voice.

She stood up and did a little pace of her own around the carpet, avoiding the man who now stood close to the steps that led into the garden.

'Look, this is an embarrassing thing to have to ask and I am ashamed to have to ask it, but if I stay, could I talk to you about some wages? Originally it was just to be two days—fly over with Samarah and fly back—then the stopover and now her niece isn't here to take over... We'd become friends, Samarah and I, and I was happy to be able to help, but I've this obligation—money that is paid out of my bank account regularly—and if I'm not working, not earning, if the money's not there—'

He cut her off with a wave of his hand, an abrupt movement that seemed to ward her off, although she was back on the settee now, embarrassed—no, utterly humiliated—by having to discuss money with a stranger.

'Money!' he snapped. 'Of course there'll be money. Do not worry, Dr Conroy, you will be well paid!'

He stalked away, his white robe swirling around him, and what felt like disgust trailing in his wake.

Not that Alex could blame him—she was pretty disgusted herself, but what else could she have done?

* * *

Anger pushed Azzam away from the woman. No, not anger so much as an irritated discomfort. At himself for not realising she *wasn't* being paid? No, the sensation seemed to have been triggered by the fact that she'd been so obviously uncomfortable at having to discuss it.

By the fact he'd made her uncomfortable?

Of course she should be paid, he'd arrange it immediately. Yet as her words replayed in his head he heard the strain behind them, particularly when she'd said 'obligation'. Now more questions arose. If the money for this obligation was paid automatically from her bank account, what good would cash be to her here?

He wheeled round, returning to find she'd walked into the garden and was moving from one rose bush to the next, smelling the blooms. The rose she held to her face now was crimson, and it brushed a little colour into her cheeks. For a moment he weakened—his irritation slipping slightly—because there was something special about the sight of that slim, jeans-clad woman standing among the roses.

'You might give your serving woman your bank

details. If, as you say, payments are taken regularly from your account, it is best I transfer the money direct into it rather than give you cash.'

'If, as I say?' she retorted, stepping away from the crimson rose and facing him, anger firing the silvery eyes. 'Do you think I'd lie to you? Or are you just trying to humiliate me further? Do you think that asking a stranger for wages wasn't humiliating enough for me? Do you think I wouldn't care for Samarah out of fondness and compassion if I didn't have financial obligations? Believe me, if I'd had an alternative, I'd have taken it.'

She stormed away, her body rigid with the force of her anger as she slapped her feet against the paving stones.

There'd been a ring of truth in her words, and the anger seemed genuine, and for a moment he regretted upsetting her. But Bahir's death had brought back too many reminders of Clarice's arrival in their midst, and suspicion was a bitter seed that flourished in pain and grief.

She shouldn't have asked, Alex told herself as, on shaking legs, she escaped the man.

She should have told him she had to leave immediately!

But how could she leave the gentle Samarah when she was grieving and ill? How could she, Alex, just walk away from a woman she'd come to admire and respect?

She'd *had* to ask, she reminded herself, so she may as well stop getting her knickers in a twist over it. So what if the man thought she was a mercenary female?

She kicked off her shoes with such force one of them flew across the paving, disturbing the neat rows of sandals already there. Muttering to herself, she squatted down to restore them all to order and it was there Samarah found her.

'You will eat with us this evening?' she asked in her quiet, barely accented English. 'I am afraid we have neglected you shamefully, but I was tired from the flight and slept until late in the day. In our country we pride ourselves on our hospitality. It comes from the time of our nomad ancestors, when to turn someone away from a camp in the desert might be to send them to their death.'

'I would be honoured to eat with you,' Alex told

her, standing up and studying Samarah's face, then watching her chest to check it was moving without strain. 'You are feeling all right?'

Samarah inclined her head then gave it a little shake.

'Hardly all right when my first-born is dead, but it is not the asthma that affects me. Only grief.'

She reached out and took Alex's hands.

'That you will understand for I read grief in your face as well. It is not so long since you lost someone?'

Alex turned away so she wouldn't reveal the tears that filled her eyes. It was tiredness that had weakened her so much that a few kind words from Samarah should make her want to cry. Weakness was a luxury she couldn't afford—like the pride that was still eating into her bones over her request for wages.

Samarah took her hand and led her into the building.

'I know I gave you little time to pack, but you will find clothes in the dressing room next to your bedroom and toiletries in the bathroom. We will eat in an hour. Hafa will show you the way.'

Alex thanked Samarah and followed Hafa, who had appeared silently in front of them, back to the splendid bedroom.

Clothes in the dressing room?

Alex looked down at her serviceable jeans and checked shirt, then caught up with her guide.

'Samarah mentioned clothes,' she said to Hafa. 'Are my clothes not suitable here?'

Hafa smiled at her.

'Because you are a foreigner no shame attaches to you, but I think Samarah has chosen clothes especially for you—a gift because she likes you— and she would be pleased to see you wear these things.'

'Very diplomatically put,' Alex responded, smiling at the woman, worry over her request to the 'new highness' pushed aside by the kindness of the women she was meeting.

Not to mention the thought of a shower and getting into clean clothes. Packing in a hurry, she'd grabbed her passport, a small travel pack, underwear and two clean shirts, thinking her jeans would do until she returned home. At the time, all she'd intended doing was accompanying Samarah home, but the older woman's asthma attack on the flight had frightened both of them, and Alex had realised she couldn't leave.

So she'd *have* to send her bank details to the prince, though her stomach twisted at the thought, and she felt ill remembering the contempt she'd seen in his eyes.

The same contempt she'd seen in David's eyes when she'd told him about Rob's debt and offered him back her engagement ring, certain in her heart he wouldn't take it—certain of a love he'd probably, in retrospect, never felt for her.

His acceptance of it had cut her deeply—the one man she'd been relying on for support backing away from her so quickly she'd felt tainted, unclean in some way.

But David was in the past and she had more than enough problems in the present to occupy her mind.

Inside her room, fearing she'd lose the courage to do it if she hesitated, she dug a notebook out of her handbag and scribbled down the information the prince would need to transfer the money. At the bottom she added, 'Thank you for doing this. I am sorry I had to ask.'

'This note needs to go to the prince,' she told Hafa, who took it and walked, soft-footed, out of the room, the roiling in Alex's stomach growing worse by the moment.

Forget it. Have a shower.

The thought brought a glimmer of a smile to her face and she pushed away all her doubts and worries. If the bedroom was like something out of the *Arabian Nights* then the bathroom was like something from images of the future. All stainless steel and glass and gleaming white marble, toiletries of every kind stacked on the glass shelving and a shower that sprayed water all over her body, massaging it with an intensity that had been delicious after the long flight.

She stripped off, undid her plait and brushed it out, deciding to try some of the array of shampoos that lined the shelves and wash her hair. The shampoo she chose had a perfume she didn't recognise, yet as she dried her hair she realised she'd smelt the same scent here and there around the palace, as if the carpets or tapestries were permeated with it.

She sniffed the air, liking it and trying to capture what it was that attracted her.

'It's frankincense,' Hafa told her when Alex asked about the scent. Frankincense—one of the gifts carried by the wise men! Again the unreality of the situation hit her—this was truly a strange and fascinating place.

By this time she was showered and dressed, in long dark blue trousers and a matching tunic top—the least noticeable set of clothing she'd found among an array of glittering clothes in the dressing room—and Hafa had returned to take her to dinner.

'I've heard of it, of course, but I don't think I've ever smelt it,' Alex said, and Hafa smiled.

'It is special to us,' she replied, but didn't explain any more than that, simply leading Alex out of the suite of rooms and along new corridors.

What seemed like a hundred women were gathered in a huge room, most of them seated on carpets on the floor, a great swathe of material spread across the floor in front of them, the material loaded with silver and brass platters piled high with fruit and nuts.

Hafa led Alex to where Samarah sat at what would be the head if there were a table. Samarah waved her to sit down beside her, greeting Alex with a light touch of her hands, clasping both of Alex's hands together.

'Tomorrow we will bury my son, my Bahir,' Samarah told her, her voice still hoarse with the tears she must have shed in private. 'You would feel out of place in the traditional ceremony so Hafa will look after you, but tonight we celebrate his existence—his life—and for this you must join us.'

'I am honoured,' Alex told her, and she meant it, for although she'd only known Samarah a short time, she'd heard many tales about this beloved son.

Serving women brought in more silver plates, placing one in front of each of the seated women, then huge steaming bowls of rice, vegetables and meat appeared, so many dishes Alex could only shake her head. Samarah served her a little from each dish, urging her to eat, using bread instead of cutlery.

'We do eat Western style with knives and forks as you do,' she explained, 'but tonight is about tradition.'

And as the meal progressed and the women began to talk, their words translated quietly by a young woman on Alex's other side, she realised how good such a custom was, for Bahir was remembered with laughter and joy, silly pranks he'd played as a boy, mistakes he'd made as a teenager, kindnesses he'd done to many people.

It was as if they talked to imprint the memories of him more firmly in their heads, so he wouldn't ever be really lost to them, Alex decided as she wandered through the rose garden when the meal had finished.

She'd eaten too much to go straight to bed, and the garden with its perfumed beauty had called to her. Now, as she walked among the roses she thought of Rob, and the bitterness she'd felt towards him since he'd taken his own life drained away. At the time she'd felt guilt as well as anger about his desperate act. She'd known he was

convinced that finding out the extent of his indebtedness had hastened their mother's death from
cancer, but Alex had been too shocked by the
extent of the debt and too devastated by David's
desertion to do more to support her brother.

Forget David—subsequent knowledge had
proved he wasn't worth being heartsick over—but
now, among the roses, she found she could think
of Rob, remembering rather than regretting. Here,
in this peaceful, beautiful place, she began to re-
construct her brother in her mind, remembering
their childhood, the tears and laughter they had
shared. Here, among the roses, she remembered
Rob's ability to make their mother laugh, even
when the burden of bringing up two children on
her own had become almost too heavy for her to
bear.

'Oh, Rob,' she whispered to the roses, and suddenly it didn't matter that she'd had to ask the
prince for money. She was doing it for Rob, and
for the wife and daughter he'd so loved—doing it
for the boy who'd shared her childhood, and had
made their mother laugh...

CHAPTER TWO

THE last person Azzam expected to find in the rose garden was the stranger, but there she was, tonight a dark shadow in the moonlight, for her fair hair was hidden by a scarf. He watched her touching rose petals with her fingertips, brushing the backs of her hands against the blooms, apparently talking to herself for he could see her lips moving.

He stepped backwards, not wanting her to see him—not wanting to have to talk to anyone— but fate decreed he missed the path, his sandal crunching on the gravel so the woman straightened and whipped round, seeming to shrink back as she caught sight of him.

'I'm sorry, maybe I shouldn't be here,' she said, and her voice sounded muted—tear filled?

'There is no reason why you shouldn't be here,' he told her, and although he'd been certain he didn't want to talk to anyone when he'd sought the solitude of the courtyard, he found himself drawn towards her.

'You like the roses?' he asked as he came closer.

'They are unbelievable,' she said, voice firmer now. 'The perfume overwhelms me. At home it's hard to find a rose with perfume. The new ones seem to have had it bred out of them. Not that we can grow roses where I live—not good ones—the humidity gives them black spot.'

Azzam found himself smiling. How disconcerting was that? Was it simply relief that all the details of the funeral were completed that he found a conversation about perfume and black spot on roses a reason to smile?

'The same humidity that triggered my mother's asthma?' he said, coming closer, smelling the perfume of the roses for himself, breathing in the scented air, releasing it slowly, relaxing, but only slightly, made wary by this unexpected shift in his mood...

She returned his smile as she said, 'That's it,' and made to move away.

He was about to put out his hand to stop her—though why he couldn't say—when she paused, turned back towards him.

'I had dinner with your mother and her women friends a little earlier,' she said quietly. 'I found it very moving that they all offered her their memories of Bahir, as if giving her gifts to help her grief. He must have been a very special person.'

Azzam knew the women gathered at this time, but offering gifts of memories? He hadn't thought of their behaviour in quite that way. He studied the woman in front of him, surprised by her perception, and caught, again, in his own memories of his twin.

'Bahir, the dazzling, the brilliant.'

The words slipped almost silently from his lips, while pain gripped his heart.

'The dazzling, the brilliant?'

The woman echoed the words and Azzam hauled his mind back into gear. He should have walked away, but perhaps talking to a stranger might ease his pain, whereas talking to his family forced him to carry theirs as well.

'It is what his name means in our language,'

he told her, and saw her shake her head as if in
wonder, then she looked up at him, her eyes a
shining silver in the moonlight.

'And your name?' she asked. 'Azzam?'

'My name is less lofty, Azzam means determined, resolute.'

Her lips curled into a smile, and it was his imagination that the ground seemed to move beneath
his feet.

'I am sure you are that,' she said. 'When your
mother spoke of you, she made it sound as if you
were the one who got things done—as if your
brother might have had the vision, but you were
the practical one who could make things happen.
She spoke of a hospital you were building—a
hospital for children.'

She was beguiling him—though it couldn't be
deliberate, for how could she have known he'd
seek refuge in the rose garden?

He set his suspicions aside as his disappointment about the hospital flooded his being and
forced words from his lips.

'It was to be a special hospital for children, built
to accommodate the families so they do not have

to be separated from their sick child. It must be a frightening place, for a child, a large, impersonal hospital, although I know these days all hospitals try to make the children's wards bright and special. In my mind it needed to be more—low set for a start, maybe two or three levels, not a towering, impersonal, corridor-littered monolith.'

'It sounds a wonderful idea,' the woman said. 'But surely you can still achieve it.'

He hesitated, uncertain why he should be discussing his dream with a stranger.

Or was it because she *was* a stranger that he found it easy to talk to her?

'I had hoped to make things happen quickly with the hospital—to make my vision come true—but having to take my brother's place as ruler will put a stop to that.'

She touched his robe above his arm and he felt the heat of her fingers sear through the fine cotton material.

'You will do it,' she said quietly. 'Determined and resolute—remember that—and although I'm sure you'll have a lot of pressing duties for a

while, surely once you're used to the job, you'll
find time for your own interests.'

'Used to the job!' He repeated the words then
laughed out loud, probably for the first time since
Bahir's death. 'You make it sound so prosaic and
just so should I be thinking. I have let all that has
happened overwhelm me.'

He took her hand and bowed to kiss it.

'Thank you, Alexandra Conroy,' he said.
'Perhaps now I shall sleep.'

Definitely weird, Alex thought as she watched
him move away, the swaying robes making it
seem as if he glided just a little above the earth.

Not the burning on her hand where he'd dropped
the casual kiss, although that *was* weird, but the
way the man had treated her, like a friend almost,
when earlier his voice had held a distinct note of
suspicion, and later, when she'd asked about the
wages, there'd been a faint note of contempt.

Yet out here in the moonlight it was as if the
afternoon's conversation had been forgotten.

Poor man, he'd be devastated by his brother's
death, and now to have to shoulder the responsibilities of the ruler—no wonder he was confused.

'*And* confusing,' she added out loud as she lifted her hand to her lips and touched them with the skin he'd kissed, the warmth his touch had generated still lingering in her body.

She smiled to herself, delighting, for a moment, in the fantasy in which she'd found herself, alone in a rose garden in a foreign country with a rivetingly handsome sheikh talking to her of his dreams...

What was she supposed to do? Alex had eaten breakfast in her room, checked on Samarah, who'd been pale but stalwart, then returned to what was coming to feel like a luxurious prison cell. Not wanting to get inadvertently caught up in the funeral proceedings, she'd stayed in her room until Hafa had explained that the ceremonies were taking place back in the city, nowhere near the palace.

Now she escaped, drawn by the compulsion of their beauty and perfume, to the rose garden. But wandering there, smelling the roses, reminded her of the strange encounter of the previous evening.

When he'd spoken of his brother, she'd felt Azzam's pain—felt it and seen it—recognising it because she'd carried a fair load of pain herself over the past few years.

Had that recognition drawn her to the man that he'd stayed in her mind, his almost stern features haunting her dreams? Or was it nothing more than the strange situation in which she found herself, making her wonder about the man and the country he was now ruling?

She wandered the courtyard, drinking in the lush beauty of it, freeing her mind of memories and questions she couldn't answer. One of the fountains spurted its water higher than the others, and she left the rose gardens to go towards it, ignoring the heat burning down from the midday sun, wanting to hear the splashing of the water and see the rainbows in its cascading descent.

As she approached it seemed to shimmer for a moment, or maybe she was still tired, for her feet faltered on the ground. Soon cries echoing from the buildings surrounding the courtyard and figures emerging out of the gloom suggested that whatever had happened wasn't tiredness or imagination.

'An earth tremor,' Hafa told Alex when she found the woman among the chattering crowd of servants who had remained at the palace. 'Sometimes we have them, though not bad earthquakes like other countries. Ours are usually gentle shivers, a reminder to people, I think, that there are powers far greater than humans can imagine. For this to happen today...well, there are people who will tell you it is the earth's response to Bahir's death—the death of a loved ruler.'

Alex considered this, wondering if it was simply accepted form that every ruler would be a loved one, or if Azzam's brother had been as dazzling and brilliant as his name.

Certain any hint of danger had passed, the women all returned to the buildings, Alex following Hafa.

'Samarah has returned,' the young woman told Alex. 'The women's part of the proceedings is done.'

'I should check on her. I still get lost—can you show me to her rooms?'

Following Hafa along the corridors, Alex felt a surge of regret that she'd probably never get to know her way around this fabulous place. Soon she'd be gone, and Al Janeen would be nothing more than a memory of a story-book bedroom and a white-robed man in a scented rose garden.

Samarah welcomed her, and although the older woman looked exhausted, her lung capacity was surprisingly good.

'See, I am better in my own land,' Samarah told her, then, to Alex's surprise, she turned and introduced a young woman who'd been hovering behind her. 'And now here is my niece, Maya. She arranged her return as soon as she heard of Bahir's death so she could care for me. But although she is now here, I would like you to stay for a while as my guest. I would like you to see something of this country that I love, and to learn a little about the people.'

Alex acknowledged the introduction, thinking she'd talk to Maya later about Samarah's condition, but right now she had to deal with her own weakness—the longing deep inside her to do exactly as Samarah had suggested, to stay and see something of this country. It was so strong, this longing, it sat like a weight on her shoulders but she couldn't stay if she wasn't needed—well, not stay and take wages, that wouldn't be right.

And she *had* to keep earning money!

Her mind was still tumbling through the ramifications of hope and obligation when she realised Maya was speaking to her.

'Adult-onset asthma?' Maya asked, holding up the folder with the information and treatment plan Alex had prepared.

'It could have been the humidity in Queensland. We've had a very hot summer and the humidity has been high,' Alex explained.

'That, and the fact that she's been debilitated since her husband's death a little over twelve months ago. I ran tests before I went away but found nothing, just a general weakening,' Maya replied. 'It was I who suggested a holiday somewhere new—somewhere she hadn't been with her husband. She was excited about it, and though I suggested a doctor should accompany her, she believed having a doctor in the group would worry her sons and, of course, *they* must be spared all worry.'

The edge of sarcasm in Maya's voice made Alex smile. Someone else wondered at Samarah's attitude towards her sons—the unstinting love that probably hid any imperfections they might have had.

An image of Azzam's striking features rose unbidden in Alex's mind.

'And now?' she asked, determinedly ignoring the image. 'Do you think she's strong enough to get through whatever will be expected of her in the weeks ahead? Is there much for her to do? Will she have duties she has to carry out?'

'More than she should have,' Maya replied, moving Alex away from the lounge on which Samarah rested. 'It is traditional that the wives of the dignitaries who have come for the funeral call on the widow, but this particular widow will make some excuse to avoid anything that might seem like work to her and Samarah will feel duty bound to take her place.'

'Perhaps the widow is just grieving too much,'

Alex offered, surprised by a hint of venom in Maya's soft voice.

'Perhaps!' Maya retorted, more than a hint this time. 'But Samarah will find the strength to do what must be done. She is a very determined woman.'

They talked a little longer about the various preventative treatments available, until Alex sensed it was time to leave. She said good-bye to Samarah, promising to see her in the morning, knowing it would be a final good-bye because staying on would be impossible.

The only bright side was that she could send a note to Azzam telling him to forget about the wages, although she'd already been gone three days and if it took a day to arrange a flight and another day to fly home, that made six by the time she got back to work. One week's wages lost, that was all.

She sighed, thinking how little importance she'd once have placed on one week's pay. These days she knew to the last cent how much was in her account, her mind doing the calculations of credit and debit automatically. Knowing what went in each week and what went out made it easy, but losing a week's pay from the two jobs would eat into the small reserve she'd been carefully hoarding.

If the clinic *did* take her back, all would be well.

And if it didn't? If they'd replaced her?

She sighed and knew she wouldn't send a note to the prince. If the job was gone, she'd need a little extra to tide her over until she found something else...

Damn it all! Why was money such a difficulty?

Gloomily Alex followed Hafa back to her room. It wasn't only for the money she had to return home. Simply put, there was no reason for her to stay. But the thought of leaving the place Samarah had spoken of with such vivid words and so obvious a love without ever seeing more of it than a highway and the high-walled building in which she was staying caused disappointment so strong in Alex that it shocked her.

Not that she *could* go home! Not right now anyway. The prince—Azzam—had said it would be arranged, but he'd hardly be organising her flight home while attending the all-day ceremonial duties of his brother's funeral, and the state visits that Maya suggested would come after it.

Needing to escape to consider these contrary reactions—wanting to stay yet knowing she couldn't—Alex retired to her room. But once there, she was uncertain what to do. She didn't want to sleep again. All the rules of air travel suggested fitting into the local time patterns as quickly as possible, so she'd go to bed at the regular time—Al Janeen time—tonight.

Now the women and maybe the men as well were back at the palace. If she went outside again—to walk around the beautiful courtyard—she might unwittingly offend. So exploration within the walls of her suite was all that remained to her. She opened cupboard doors, discovering a small writing desk, and behind another door a television set. Wondering if the funeral procedures might be televised, she turned it on, not understanding any of the words but guessing from the serious expression of the news-reader that he could be talking of the ceremony.

Huge photos of a man so like Azzam he *had*
to be Bahir appeared to have been erected all
along the street, and shots of them were flash-
ing across the screen, interspersed with images
of a crowd, no doubt lingering from the funeral.
White-garbed men and women, a sea of white,
filled the screen, and their cries of grief echoed
from the television set, filling the room with their
pain.

With the voice droning on in the background,
Alex sat at the desk, taking up a pen and finding
paper, determined to jot down her meagre impres-
sions of this country she had yet to see.

And probably never would!

She'd barely begun to write when a change
in the tone of the talking head's voice had her
turning back towards the screen. Once again she
couldn't understand the words, but now a map
was showing on the screen, apparently a map of
Al Janeen. The capital—given the airport and the
lights, Alex assumed they were somewhere near
it—was shown in the bottom right of the picture,
and arrows pointed to an area to the north.

'Great! They're probably being invaded!' she

muttered to herself. 'Don't coups usually happen when the monarchy is unstable—when there's a change of ruler? Just my luck to be caught in a war in a foreign country! What else can happen?'

Wanting to know more—the timbre of the man's voice suggested shock and panic—but still worried that if she wandered beyond the building she might end up where she shouldn't be, Alex left her room, wondering where Hafa disappeared to when she didn't need her.

Hafa was sitting outside the door, legs crossed, head bent over some intricate embroidery.

She smiled as she stood up and tucked the piece of material into her pocket.

'I wonder if you could explain something else to me,' Alex asked. 'I turned on the television in my room and the announcer sounded very excited about something happening in the north of your country. Is it a war?'

'A war?' the young woman repeated, looking more puzzled than anxious by the question. 'I do not think war. We are a peaceful country and we like and respect our neighbours.'

'Come and see,' Alex invited and led her back

to her room where the television still showed a map of what Alex assumed was Al Janeen, with arrows pointing to a place in the north.

Hafa listened for a while, a frown gathering, marring her fine, clear skin.

'It is not war but an earthquake,' she said, still frowning. 'This is not good. The town is a not big one, more a village really, but it is a very old place of history in the north, between the mountains, and the reports are saying the quake was very severe.'

'That must have been the tremor we felt here,' Alex remembered. 'I was in the garden.'

The young woman nodded but she was obviously too engrossed in what she was hearing from the television to be taking much notice of Alex.

'Many people have been injured,' Hafa explained. 'There is a school that has collapsed with children inside. The town is in the mountains and landslides have closed the roads in and out, so it will be hard to get help and supplies to it.'

She paused as a new figure appeared on the screen, a familiar figure.

'It is His Highness, His new Highness,' she

pointed out, her relief so evident Alex had to wonder at the man's power. 'He has left his brother's funeral. He says he will go there now. If the helicopter cannot land, he has been lowered from one before. He will assess the situation and arrange to bring in whatever is needed. He can also give immediate medical help.'

'Where will he go from?' Alex asked, as new excitement stirred inside her. This was what she'd been trained for, but it was some time since she'd done this kind of work, the need to earn as much as possible to repay Rob's debts taking precedence over all else.

'He will fly from here—his own helicopter is here at the palace. It is used for rescues as well as his private business so it has medical equipment on board. Sometimes it takes people to hospital if there is an emergency. It brought the other Highness, Prince Bahir, to the hospital after the accident.'

Alex had heard enough. What she had to do was find Azzam and offer her services—explain her training and expertise, not to mention her experience.

But finding Azzam might not be the best way to attack this situation. Better by far to find the helicopter and get aboard. Samarah was in good hands with Maya. The hospital would already be on full alert. Arrangements would be under way for other medical staff to get to the stricken area, but she knew from experience that such arrangements took time, while the sooner trained people were in place, the more chance there was of saving the injured.

She wrapped a scarf around her head—downdraughts from helicopters caused havoc with even braided long hair. The helicopter, if it was used for rescues, would have emergency equipment on board, but she grabbed a small plastic pack out of her hand luggage. In it she had waterless hand cleaner, a small toothbrush and toothpaste, a spare pair of undies and a tiny manicure set—experience in emergencies had taught her to be prepared. The pack fitted easily into the wide pockets of her loose trousers. Then she ran out the door, calling to Hafa to show her the way.

CHAPTER THREE

'YOU are doing what?'

Azzam stared in disbelief when he saw Alex already strapped into the back of the helicopter, adjusting a helmet over her pale hair.

'Coming with you to the earthquake region,' she answered calmly, adding, too quickly for him to argue, 'and before you get uptight about it, it's what I'm trained to do. As well as clinic work, I'm an ER doctor, mostly doing night shifts these days, but I'm a specialist major emergency doctor with experience of triage in cyclones, fire and floods. I also know how long it takes to get hospital personnel mobilised, and right now, for the people in that village, two doctors are better than one, so let's go.'

Was she for real?

Surely she wouldn't be lying about experience

like that, and if she wasn't lying, she'd certainly be useful.

'Maya is with your mother, so she is in good hands.'

She *sounded* genuine, and he knew from his mother that she appeared to genuinely care, but he must have still looked doubtful for she hurried on.

'I've been lowered from helicopters. I've done rescues off ships. I *am* trained.'

'Cutting my legs out from under me—isn't that the expression?' he responded.

She smiled and he realised it was only the second time he'd seen a proper smile from her, but this one, in daylight rather than the dim light of the rose garden, was something special. Her generous lips curved in what seemed like genuine delight, while silver flashes danced in her eyes.

Disturbed in ways he didn't want to think about, he turned away from her, gave a curt order to his pilot, nodded to the navigator, who would act as winchman if necessary, and climbed into the front seat. He hoped there'd be a patch of flat land where the helicopter could land, but if there wasn't they'd have to be lowered on a cable.

'You say you've been winched down on a cable?' he asked, speaking through the microphone in his helmet as the engines were roaring with the power needed for lift-off.

'Onto the deck of a ship pitching in sixty-knot winds,' she told him, and he felt an urge to grind his teeth.

'Wonder-woman, in fact?' he growled instead.

She glanced his way and shrugged.

'No, but I believe if you're going to do something you should do it well.'

He believed the same thing himself, so it couldn't be that causing his aggravation. Was it nothing more than the presence of the woman in the helicopter?

Impossible question to answer, so he turned to practical matters, taking care to keep any hint of sarcasm out of his voice as he said, 'Well, you've probably had experience of this before, but unless the chopper lands a fair distance away, dust from the rotors can cause more problems for people who have been injured, or buried beneath the rubble. Dropping in a short distance away is usually safer and if we can establish a drop zone, medical supplies and water can be lowered into the same place as well.'

Azzam realised he'd mostly done training runs and learnt from books and lectures the latest ways to handle mass disasters. He'd even written the hospital's policy papers for the management of such things. But he'd never really expected it to happen—not in his own country.

Driven by his need to see for himself, and his fear for the people of the northern village, he'd left the funeral feast and rushed straight back to his rooms, issuing orders through the phone to the hospital as he went, speaking to the police department and army officers as he changed into tough outdoor wear, making sure the emergency response teams he had set up, but never yet used, were all springing into action.

'I don't know how long the flight will take, but you should try to snatch some sleep.' Her voice broke into his thoughts as he went over the arrangements he'd already put in place.

'Sleep?'

He heard the word echo back in his helmet and realised he'd spoken a bit abruptly.

'I've found these emergency situations are a bit like being back in our intern years, and the rule is the same—snatch what sleep you can when you can.'

He realised she was right. There was nothing else to do until they were on the ground, where, together, they would assess the situation and call in whatever help was needed.

He wanted to tell her she was right and that he was grateful to her for being there, grateful that he'd have someone with whom to discuss the situation and work out best options, but it had been a long time since he'd shared any feelings with a stranger—and a female stranger at that.

Yet—

'I *will* sleep.'

At least he'd acknowledged her presence, Alex thought as she looked around the interior of the helicopter. She sat in one of two seats fitted against the fuselage, a door beside her and another one opposite it. In the seat behind the pilot, directly opposite her, was another man, who apparently

didn't speak English for he hadn't been involved
in the conversation Alex had had with the pilot
when she'd persuaded him to allow her to join
the flight.

Alex assumed this second man would play
multiple roles—second pilot, navigator, and
winchman.

She hoped he was good at his job!

Secured to the walls were familiar-looking
equipment backpacks. Some would hold emergency medical supplies, one a special defibrillator
and vital-signs monitor. Next to them were two
collapsible stretchers, also in backpacks, and she
could see where these, once opened out, could be
secured to the floor of the aircraft.

'I understood this was your personal chopper,
so why the emergency equipment?' she said, for-
getting she'd told her companion to sleep.

'It *is* the prince's aircraft, he flies it himself at
times,' the pilot replied, 'but he believes it should
have more use than a convenience to get him to
and from work in the city, so he had it specially
fitted out.'

Knowing how much money was needed to keep

the emergency helicopter services afloat at home,
Alex could only marvel that one person could
have a private aircraft like this at his disposal. Her
wages would be chicken feed to him, although
even thinking about her request for wages made
her stomach squirm.

Forget it! she told herself, and she did, turning
instead to peer out the window, seeing for the
first time what a desert looked like.

It was like flying over the sea at sunset, something she'd been lucky enough to do, seeing the
ocean turned to red-gold, the row upon row of
waves like the dunes beneath them now. But shadows were already touching the eastward sides of
the dunes and the blackness of those shadows
made the colours more vivid.

Up ahead she could see mountains rising from
the sands—red mountains with deeper shadows below them, what appeared to be a road or
track of some kind disappearing between two
ranges.

Used to flying over coastal scenes and green-
ery and water, the endless red conjured up the
magic-carpet image yet again, the patterns of the

windswept sand and shadows like the patterns in the carpets back at the palace or whatever it was to which she'd been taken.

'Ayee!'

The cry came from the man behind the pilot and Alex peered forward, shocked by what had caused his cry. From the air it looked as if large white blocks had been tumbled down a hill but, as they drew closer, Alex realised they were houses.

'It is a narrow ravine,' Azzam explained, his bleary voice suggesting he had slept at least for a short time. 'It was a guard point on an ancient trade route—the frankincense trade, in fact. It was settled because of the oasis there at the bottom, the houses built on the sides of the hills because the *wadi*—the river bed—floods after rain.'

His voice faded from her earphones but not before Alex had heard shock and deep sadness in it.

Now Alex could see where the mountain looked as if it had sheared in two—as if some giant with a mighty sword had sliced through it. She was trying to make sense of it when the helicopter lifted in the air, turning away from the shattered remains of the town and heading back along the narrow valley.

'We could cause more disruption with the noise so we will winch down further along the valley,' Azzam said to her. He had climbed into the back cabin and looked directly into Alex's face.

'There is no need for you to do this,' he said, the dark eyes so intent on hers she felt a shiver of apprehension down her spine.

'I didn't come along for the ride,' she told him, unbuckling her seat belt and standing as steadily as she could. 'Which backpack do you want me to take?'

His eyes studied her again, assessing her.

'The medical supplies and stretchers can drop safely, but I would appreciate it if you would take the defibrillator. I don't anticipate needing it but the monitor could be handy. The pilot will drop us in, lower what gear he can, then return to the capital to bring back more personnel and supplies. He will find a safe place to land further down the valley and the rescuers can walk in. For now I—we—need to assess the damage and get word out about the amount of damage done and the kind of help we will need.'

Alex took the small backpack he passed her.

'Strap it on your front,' Azzam told her. 'We will be winched down together.'

Alex stared at him.

'I've *been* winched down before, I *know* the routine!'

'Together,' the infuriating man repeated, while Alex added 'bossy and obstinate' to the meanings of his name.

It was an exercise drop, nothing more, she told herself as Azzam's strong arms closed around her. And she was only annoyed because he didn't trust her to do it on her own!

More annoyed because she felt uncomfortable about the way he was holding her, as if dangling on a line above an earthquake-wrecked valley was some kind of romantic foreplay!

Yet annoyance couldn't mask the responses of her body, which, through clothes and backpack straps and webbing, still felt the hardness of the man who held her clamped against him.

Still reacted to it, warming so inappropriately she wondered if she was blushing.

Would she have felt this reaction with David holding her? Or was it because she'd known him so well she'd never felt these tingling, tightening sensations along her nerves, or a strange heaviness in her muscles, when *he'd* held her in his arms.

David had only ever kissed her, nothing more. Anything extra was what he'd kept for the string of other women who, unbeknownst to Alex at the time, had drifted in and out of her fiancé's life.

'Ready to roll if we need to?' Azzam asked, his chin brushing her ear, the words so close she felt as well as heard them. She drew up her knees, unconsciously pressing closer to him so they'd roll together as they hit the ground. But the roll wasn't needed, the helicopter pilot holding the craft steady and the winchman easing them onto the ground so they stepped from the loop in the cable without even the slightest jar.

Azzam released the line and moved away from his companion, disturbed by the fact his body had responded to hers, not boldly or obviously but with a flare of awareness that was totally inappropriate. He'd not been with a woman for some time, preferring to keep his life distraction free as he'd pushed ahead with his plans for the children's hospital—*his* hospital. At first it had been little more than a wild idea—a hospital purely for children, staffed only by specialist paediatric doctors and nurses. He could have, as Bahir had pointed out many times, simply built a special wing onto the existing hospital, but Azzam was certain the new hospital would provide a more peaceful and positive atmosphere for families from a culture that had an inbred fear and dread of being separated from their children.

The woman who'd been the source of his body's betrayal was looking up towards the cradle stretcher being lowered from the chopper, the basket laden with more medical supplies. She lifted her arms to catch it as it drew close and he stepped up beside her, taking it from her.

'Stand clear, I will do it,' he said—or maybe ordered.

She snapped a salute at him and said, 'Yes, sir!' in a derisive tone that would have earned instant retribution in his army. Did she not realise who he was?

The thought had no sooner swung into his mind—as he swung the stretcher to the ground—than he had to shake his head at the impertinence of it. There *were* some women in Al Janeen's army now, and he supposed it *was* his army, but *this* woman was here to help his country. He could hardly bust her for insubordination!

'I am grateful to you for coming here,' he said, straightening up and looking directly at her. 'I may not have said that before.'

She smiled, the smile that had struck him as unusual once before, and he caught the glint in her eyes again.

'No, you may not have,' she agreed. 'Now, shall we leave most of this gear here until we've seen what we're up against? I think even the defibrillator could stay and I'll carry the second pack of medical supplies.'

He took the defibrillator from her and fitted it onto his chest, then held the pack of medical supplies as she put her arms through the straps. He adjusted them for her slight frame and was about to secure them across her breasts when the inappropriate heat he'd felt earlier returned.

Tiredness, grief, concern over what they would find in the village…

No wonder his head was no longer in control of his body. And if he was going to be attracted to a woman, it certainly couldn't be to this woman. His brother's experience of marriage had been enough to convince Azzam to seek a wife— something, given the circumstances, he'd have to do before long—from his own country, someone who knew what would be involved in her duties and would carry them out without a fuss.

'Right, let's go,' said the woman to whom he wasn't attracted, the pack securely strapped across the breasts he'd come close to touching.

The downdraught from the helicopter as they were lowered had loosened her head scarf and she was retying it as she spoke. He watched as she covered the pale hair and wondered about a woman who would voluntarily come to help people she didn't know.

Of course, she was a doctor, but would all doctors have reacted in this way?

Might not some have offered to help out at the hospital?

What motivated such a woman?

She was here to help and then she'd leave, so all he could do was wonder.

He finished strapping his two backpacks into place and looked up, realising she was well ahead of him, striding out along the old track at the bottom of the valley.

And for some obscure reason the fact that he wouldn't get to know her well caused a twinge of something that felt very like regret deep inside him.

None of the buildings had been very big, Alex realised as she drew closer to the scene of devastation that lay before her, but as they'd tumbled down the steep-sided hills on either side of the valley they'd crushed the buildings below them.

Azzam joined her and she read on his face the same pain and horror she was feeling, although for him, she knew, it must go deeper, for these were his people.

'Daytime,' he groaned. 'The school would have

been operating. It was there, tucked beneath the cliff on the lower level.'

He pointed across the rift.

'And the market, a little further on, would have been full of men and women, traders and customers.'

They were close now, opposite where he'd pointed out the school, and they could see dust-covered figures working in the rubble and hear the cries of panicked men and women, no doubt parents of the children who lay beneath the shattered walls and roof.

'You go on ahead,' Alex said. 'You need to see the whole picture before you can radio out for more help. I'll stay here and tend the rescued.'

He turned and frowned at her, as if he couldn't understand her words.

'Go!' she ordered. 'The sooner you report back to the services in the city, the sooner we'll have more help.'

'But I cannot expect you—'

Azzam was trying to work out which was the most important reason for his not leaving her—safety, danger from an aftershock, her lack of understanding of the language—when she spoke again.

'Go,' she repeated, and, knowing she was right, he went, his heart growing heavier and heavier in his chest as he saw the extent of the destruction and heard the wailing cries of the injured and bereft.

The village headman came to greet him, blackened streaks of tears tattooed by grief and horror on his cheeks.

'Highness, you have come,' the man said, taking one of Azzam's hands in both of his, then, speaking quickly, he explained what was already being done, pointing to where a line of men and women lifted and passed back jagged rocks and pieces of mud-brick wall from the top of the debris, digging down to find the injured.

Azzam walked what was left of the village with him, before radioing back to the hospital at Al Janeen, which he'd already established as the control point for all services. The first necessity was for a helicopter to drop bottled water and more medical supplies, also paramedics and the small group of trained army rescue specialists. Heavy equipment should be sent along the road to clear the landslide there, so ambulances and supply vehicles could get through. In the meantime, they'd airlift out the most seriously injured people, but night was closing in quickly in this deep valley, the darkness making it too dangerous for a helicopter to come in low, so no more help would be arriving tonight.

The cries of the children beneath the rubble tore at Alex's heart and she dug into it, working as fast as the men and women already there, tearing away the rocks but careful all the time that they didn't cause any further collapse for the cries told them the children—at least some of them—were alive.

'Aiyiyi!'

The high-pitched wail startled her, but it had the quality of happiness rather than grief. She hurried to the man who was crying out, and saw him squat, pointing downward.

'Doctor—I'm a doctor—medico,' she said, hoping one of the words would ring a bell with someone in the group.

It must have, for the man moved to squat a little farther away, passing Alex a torch so she could shine it into a gap that had appeared beneath a huge slab of wall.

The torchlight picked up two shining eyes, a grubby face and lips twisted in pain or fear.

'Talk to the child,' she said to the man. 'Do you understand me?'

'I know little English. I talk. What more?'

'Ask if there are other children there.'

The man took the torch and moved into her place, and Alex mentally congratulated him as his voice was calm and soothing as he spoke into the darkness.

'More children,' he reported back to her, 'but they can't get out.'

Alex studied the pile of stones and rubble they would need to shift, wondering just how stable it might be. Once they pulled more rocks off the top, might that not alter a precarious balance and cause the lot to collapse on the children?

Tentatively she moved a rock that was beneath the slab but not supporting anything, then another, until she had a hole she knew she could slide into.

'I will go down and pass the children up to you,' she told the English-speaking man.

He wailed in horror, throwing up his hands then passing on the information to the gathered men and women, who now clustered closer to Alex, speaking rapidly but whether in delight that she was going to rescue their children or warning her not to do it, she didn't know. She only knew they accentuated the danger.

'Tell them to keep right back—right off the rubble—and don't move any more stones until I get the children out.'

She wasn't sure if his English was good enough, but the man not only understood but obeyed immediately—waving the people back onto firm ground, yelling at those who hesitated even momentarily, moving them all back to a safe distance.

She removed her backpack and opened it, showing the man whom she'd appointed as her helper what was in it. She unwrapped the webbing from the pack, knowing the backstraps could be used as a rope, and indicated she would take one end down the hole as she went.

'I'd prefer to pass the children up to you,' she said. 'The rope might help the older ones climb. When they come out, there are three things you must check, ABC, airways, breathing, circulation. Clear the mouth and nose of dust or debris, make sure the child is breathing, or breath for him or her.'

Alex used a rock to demonstrate breathing into a child's mouth and nose.

'Then check the heartbeat and find any blood. If it's pumping out—' she used her hands to illustrate a spray of blood '—apply a tight pad and bandage over it.'

The man nodded, repeating 'ABC' as if the concept was familiar to him.

With the medical supplies set out and the agitated crowd safely out of the way—if there *was* a collapse she didn't want anyone else injured—she had to figure out the easiest way into the space where the children were trapped. Feet first for sure, but on her back or on her belly?

'Do not even think about it!'

Azzam's voice came from directly behind her, and she turned, sure he must be speaking to her because who else would speak such perfect English?

'You cannot go down there.'

'Of course I can,' she told him, irritated by the waste of time an argument would cause and knowing from his voice that argument was looming. 'Look at the hole—I'm the only one who will fit. Besides, you'll be more useful up here tending the injured—you can ask questions and understand the answers the injured people give you, which is more than I can do.'

She didn't wait for his response, opting to slide in on her belly, thinking she could remove any impediments beneath her without compromising what was above. Tremors of fear vibrated along her nerves as she knotted the wide trousers around her ankles so they wouldn't impede her. She reminded herself that one of the reasons she'd become involved in rescue work had been to overcome her fear of small, enclosed spaces—a fear she refused to acknowledge as claustrophobia.

Wriggling down a short tunnel that seemed to

have the dimensions of a rabbit burrow, she finally reached a place where most of her body was dangling in the air, only her head still in the hole, with her arms above it, braced against the sides so she wouldn't plummet to the floor and injure some small child.

Above her she could hear Azzam's voice, still grumbling and growling, but her entire being was focussed now on what lay below.

Were there older children in the space? Would they have the sense to keep the younger ones out of her way when she fell?

She was still wondering about this when small hands grasped her leg and she found her feet guided onto something. A rock? Perhaps a desk?

Praying that it would take her weight, she released the pressure of her arms against the rock tunnel and eased herself out, turning on the torch she'd thrust into her pocket before starting her journey. She was standing on what must have been the teacher's table, a solid wooden piece of furniture that right now seemed like an enormous piece of luck.

Shining the torch around, she saw dark eyes, most red with tears, peering at her out of dusty, blood-streaked faces. She dropped down off the desk and held out her arms. The little bodies crowded against her, so, for a few seconds, they could feel the safety of an adult hug.

'English?' she asked, but there was no response, so she eased herself away from them and lined them up, running the torch over each child, checking for serious injury. She had reached the end of the line of nine when she saw the others on the floor, some sitting, some lying down, perhaps unconscious.

She was drawn towards these children that needed help, perhaps immediately, but instinct yelled at her to get the others out. Perhaps she could do both.

Checking the line-up, she chose the smallest child and, lifting the little girl onto the table, she climbed up, tied the webbing around her, and lifted her higher into the hole. Alex tugged the rope and felt an answering tug. The little one would suffer scrapes being hauled up the short but rough tunnel, but at least they were fixable.

Next she chose a sturdy-looking boy and, as soon as the feet of the small girl disappeared from view, she pointed to the tunnel and made climbing motions with her hands. The boy understood and as soon as she held him up, he grasped at stones on the sides of the escape route and climbed nimbly out of sight.

The children, realising what was happening, began to clamour, no doubt about who would be next. Another big child climbed onto the table as the rope slithered back down. He gesticulated to the hole and to the children then pointed at Alex and at the patients in the corner.

Without words Alex understood he would do her job of lifting the children while she tended the injured, so she climbed down, passed him a small child, and, not wanting him to think she didn't trust him to save his friends, turned her attention to the children on the floor.

Not all of them were children, she realised, for a man in a long, dark robe lay there as well, his body curled protectively around the smallest of the injured. He was dead, Alex saw at once, but the child beneath him was alive. He'd saved that child!

She'd left her torch on the desk so all the children had some light to lift their fears, and couldn't see what injuries these—four, she counted—had suffered. Not wanting to deprive the children of the light, she'd have to go by feel, and trust her hands to do the basic diagnosis. Chest first to check on breathing and heartbeat—rapid movement. This child was alive. Her hands felt their way to the head, seeking a tell-tale shift in the bony skull, feeling for blood spurting or seeping. No head wound but further exploration revealed this first child had an open fracture of the humerus, no doubt the pain of that contributing to the child's lack of consciousness.

Aware there could be spinal damage but more concerned about further injury should an aftershock bring down the wall above where they lay, she lifted the child and carried him across the small space, placing him beneath the table in the hope—possibly false—that its solidity might provide some protection.

One of the children waiting to be lifted out

began to cry and knelt beside the child. No doubt a sibling, a bond so strong the able child was obviously insisting she stay too, settling beneath the table to hold the little boy's hand.

No time to argue! Alex shrugged at her helper on the table and passed another child up to him. Five to go, then him, then the injured ones. She'd need to work out how best to get them out.

The next child was conscious, anxious eyes peering at her in the dim light, lips moving as he tried to tell Alex something. His breathing was okay, heart rate rapid but not dangerously so, no sign of bleeding, but when Alex pricked the small foot with a sharp shard of plaster she'd found on the floor, the little boy didn't flinch. Spinal injury. How was she supposed to handle that?

She crossed to the table again and took the torch.

'Sorry, kids,' she said, although she knew they wouldn't understand, and she swept the torchlight around the small space, searching for anything that might do to stabilise the injured boy's neck and spine. A tall stick stood in one corner. With these steep hills, maybe the teacher had used it as a walking aid. She grabbed it and returned the torch to the table so the evacuation could continue, but before she could break the stick, she heard a voice yelling down the tunnel.

'That was an aftershock! Are you all right? Come up out of there—we'll extend the hole.'

CHAPTER FOUR

AZZAM held his breath. How could he have been so stupid as to leave Alex on her own? Although he could hardly have known she'd decide to go down through an impossibly small hole into the ground below. She was either incredibly brave or incredibly foolish, but he could no longer hover here above her while she risked her life in an unstable hole beneath the ground.

Surely they could enlarge the hole.

'Nothing shifted,' she called up to him, sounding so calm and composed he regretted the momentary panic he'd felt as the ground had shuddered once more. 'But there is something you could do. There are no children in the tunnel right now so could you drop down some bandages, and a small neck collar if there's one in the pack, a couple of splints if you have them. Most of those men are wearing intricate turbans—could you drop a few of them down too so I can use them as bindings to protect the injured children as you pull them out?'

Calm and composed? She was more than that. Thinking ahead and thinking clearly—thinking medically.

'And another torch,' she called. 'That should provide weight for the other things as you drop them.'

'Get out and let me come down,' he ordered.

'As if you'd fit,' she retorted. 'Just get that stuff down here so I can get the rest of these kids out. This space could disappear if there's another aftershock.'

The image she'd offered him stopped his heart for a moment, but he organised what she needed, grumbling to himself all the time, frustrated that this stranger was doing so much for his people— that *she* should be the one risking her life. She was a visitor to his country—a guest—and she had put her life in danger.

It wasn't right!

And yet it was. As she'd said, she'd trained for

it—it was what she did—but the courage it must have taken for her to slide down that hole...

'Some time soon,' she prompted, and he bundled up the things he'd been putting together as his mind raced with worry. Thinking ahead, as she had, he realised she might need more than a few turbans. He slid off his gown and wrapped that around the bundle, and dropped it down.

Alex heard a lot of grumbling from above but eventually a bundle came down the hole, wrapped not in black turban material but in dirty white cloth which she suspected had once been Azzam's pristinely perfect gown. An image of the man ungowned—broad chest, toned abs—flashed into her head but was quickly banished. For all she knew, he could have a pigeon chest and a beer gut.

Obviously her brain was using these irrelevancies to stop her worrying about the situation. She lifted a little girl who had become hysterical and was flailing in her arms, making it obvious she had no intention of being thrust up into the hole above their temporary shelter. Using the dark turbans, Alex wrapped the little limbs so the child's arms were close to her body and her legs bound together, not too tightly but not loosely enough for the child to kick or hit out and injure herself against the tunnel wall.

Using the webbing, she tied her bundle securely then called up to Azzam.

'As far as I can tell, this child is uninjured but she's panicking so I've wrapped her in a bundle. Can you haul her gently? Are the children's parents out there? Is there someone who can soothe the poor wee thing?'

Azzam felt the tug on the webbing rope and pulled gently, finding, indeed, a bundle on the end of it. Alex had managed to swaddle the little girl so completely that even her face was covered with a thin layer of cloth through which loud shrieks of fear and anger could still be heard.

Anxious hands took the bundle from him, the child passed back from man to man until it reached the parents waiting on the solid ground at the base of the *wadi*. The loud wailing cry of a woman told him the child had found her mother, but again his attention was drawn back to the hole.

The work continued, bigger children scrambling out on their own, smaller ones wrapped and tied to the webbing.

'The boy coming up next is a hero,' Alex called to him. 'It is he who looked after the other children and then passed them up to the hole so they could get out. But I think he's close to exhaustion so if you could reach in to help him out, I would be grateful.'

'*You* would be grateful!' Azzam muttered, but mostly to himself as he flattened himself on the rough ground and eased his head and arms into the hole, hoping to feel for the boy's hands and haul him out.

The hands were smaller than he'd expected, a child still, this lad.

'You are all right. You have been very brave to help the others. You are only a boy but the doctor says you did a man's job down there.' He urged the boy upward, drew him out then held him close, soothing him as he spoke, because now he was out of danger the scared child inside the lad had begun to shake and cry.

'But I need more help from you,' he added as the boy calmed down.

Hearing the conversation, a woman called from the *wadi*.

'Help the man, Dirar. He is your prince.'

The boy looked up at him.

'You are the prince?'

There was so much wonder in the boy's face, Azzam had to smile.

'But I am only a man,' he said, 'and once I was a boy like you, but I doubt I was as brave. Now, tell me, Dirar, how many people are still trapped and what is the doctor doing down there?'

'Our teacher is there but I think he is dead,' Dirar whispered, tears sliding down his cheeks again. 'And Tasnim will not come because her brother is hurt. He is under the table. The woman put him there.'

Great! Just wonderful! Azzam thought to himself. The mountain could collapse and that insane female thought a school table might provide protection.

Yet inside the anger he acknowledged respect, for she was doing the best she could under incredible and horrific circumstances. It was frustration that he couldn't be down there himself that made him want to snarl like a wild leopard.

Leopards!

Night was coming and the leopards would smell the blood of the dead and injured...

He'd think of that later. Now he had to concentrate on what the boy was telling him. Four injured children and a loyal sister. Would he and Bahir have been less foolish over women—over Clarice—if they'd grown up with sisters?

'So you must get them out now,' the boy was telling him, easing out of Azzam's arms and running nimbly over the debris of the buildings towards the waiting arms of his mother.

A tug on the rope reinforced his decision to concentrate on one thing at a time.

'I've splinted this one's arm as best I could. I notice you sent morphine down but not knowing if the child has head injuries I didn't want to use it. He's unconscious anyway. Perhaps when he comes up, you should get my English-speaking helper back there and do some doctoring.'

Did she not want him here? Azzam wondered

as he gently pulled the rope. He felt so drawn to stay—so held in place by the fear he had for her—he doubted he could move, although what she'd said made sense.

The child, again bundled like a mummy, emerged, and after the bundle a small girl scrambled out, glaring at Azzam as he unwrapped the turban from the injured child's face so he could breathe more easily.

'My brother!' she said, in such a possessive voice Azzam put out his arms and drew her into a hug.

'You are a good sister,' he told her in her own language as she wept against him. 'Your brother will be all right. I am going to pass him over to safe ground and I want you to go with him.'

The little girl nodded against his shoulder but even after she eased away he felt the imprint of her frail body.

Would the day ever come when he could put the past behind him, and hug his own children?

It would have to come. The country would need an heir...

'It'll be a while before I can move the rest,' a

soft voice called, recalling him yet again to his duty. And loath though he was to leave the top of the escape hatch, he waved to the man who'd held the position earlier and they crossed paths as he made his way down to the *wadi* to see the injured child. Dr Conroy—he'd think of her that way—was right. There were already too many injured people to be tended by one doctor. He'd had no business to be wasting time in the rescue effort.

The villagers were lining the injured up on a grassy bank near where the *wadi* had been deepened and widened to form an oasis. On this section of the northern side there'd been no buildings to collapse so the area was safe from anything but a rock fall and he had to pray that wouldn't happen until the road was clear and all the injured evacuated.

Men had walked back to the helicopter drop and carried the cradle with supplies, and some of the women were carrying bottles of water to the men still lifting debris. Azzam concentrated on the victims, seeing first the little boy with the broken arm, checking the rough way Alexandra

had positioned the splints and wrapped them, realising she'd been trying to immobilise the arms
so the movement up the escape route wouldn't
cause further damage.

What to do? The child was conscious now,
asking for his mother, his sister by his side. He
was breathing easily and didn't seem to be in
much pain. He could be dealt with later—decisions made then about setting the arm.

He wanted to tell the little girl to find their
mother, but what if their mother was trapped? Did
he want to send the child on a search that could
cause her heartbreak?

He patted her head instead, telling her to watch
her brother—an unnecessary statement as she
seemed to have attached herself to his good hand
and had no intention of moving.

Azzam walked towards the other injured villagers, thinking only of lifesaving measures, knowing he needed to prioritise who would be lifted
out first and who could be cared for here.

'Sir, sir!'

A call from the man at the school. Azzam hurried back and was handed a small form wrapped

in his once-white gown. The child's pulse was faint, so Azzam carried him swiftly to the *wadi* and put him gently on the ground, carefully unwrapping the little form, finding not only a brace around the child's neck but three lengths of stick ingeniously bound into a firm stretcher, the little body tied to it with lengths of turban.

Azzam grabbed a torch from the pack and opened one of the child's eyes to shine the light into it. No response. Neither was there any response when he pinched a finger or a toe.

A woman dropped to her knees beside the child, demanding that he sit up, refusing to accept the child might be badly injured, berating Azzam for not helping her son to sit.

'Spinal injury or brain, internal injury, it's hard to tell,' a soft voice said, and he realised the rescuer had been rescued. She was filthy, her clothes torn and her hands streaked with blood, yet his heart gave a leap that he knew was relief that she was safe, for all it was an unusual response. 'I think he is the most severely injured, although there's a little girl who's comatose as well. I brought her out. Her father is with her.'

She hesitated, then added, 'The school teacher and another child are both dead. It would be good to get them out so they can be laid to rest by their families, but I thought I might be needed here.'

He could hear the anxiety in her voice and understood she'd fought a battle with herself before leaving those two souls behind.

'You did the right thing,' he assured her. 'And you saved the other children as well, remember that, although—' his voice deepened to a growl '—your behaviour was incredibly foolhardy.'

Not that she took the slightest notice of him, turning to wash her hands with water from a bottle then kneeling beside a woman who'd been pulled from the rubble.

Alex checked and re-checked the injured, one by one, doing what she could for each of them in these appalling circumstances, aware, all the time, of the presence of Azzam, not because the local people were treating him with such deference but because some kind of awareness—definitely unwanted and totally bizarre—was tweaking at her body.

Had it started in the rose garden, this attraction?

Had she been drawn to him when he'd revealed just a little of his grief for the brother he'd so obviously loved?

Surely it couldn't be the bare chest. His lower half was decently garbed in what looked like a once-white sarong-type thing, though in the ingenious way of these people it was now fashioned into, yes, Sinbad-type trousers.

But it *was* the bare chest, olive skin, streaked with ash and dust, over heavy slabs of muscle, the chest of an athlete, not a doctor or a prince, that was causing her uneasiness. Not that she knew what princes' chests *should* look like but not many doctors she knew had time to work out sufficiently to keep such well-defined muscles.

What was she doing?

How could her mind be wandering like this— *she* who prided herself on her focus and professional competence?

She moved to the next patient, focussing all her attention on the injured.

Until she heard the cry.

'That's a baby.'

She looked over towards where the school had been, sure of what she'd heard.

'It was a bird,' Azzam told her, but already the little girl who had sat beneath the table beside her injured brother was stumbling across the wrecked buildings towards the hole.

'There couldn't have been a baby in the school,' Azzam said, patient common sense accentuating the denial. But already Alex was following the child.

'Ask her,' she called back to Azzam. 'Ask her why she knows the cry.'

Alex caught the child and passed her back to Azzam, who, although she struggled and objected loudly, held her gently and easily in his arms, calming her with his voice.

'She says her mother always came to meet them after school. She brought the baby. She says her father is away—he is gone, she says, although I don't know what she means by that.'

'They could have been outside the school—the mother and the baby. I'm going back down,' Alex told him, then saw the fury in his face as he thrust the child into someone else's arms and stepped towards her.

'I will *not* leave an infant down there!' Alex told him, hoping the defiance in her voice was visible in her face for there was no time to be arguing with this man.

'You know you won't fit and neither will any of the men I've seen here,' she added, before he had time to open his mouth for his objection. 'If you want to be useful, you can hold the rope.'

Alex eased herself feet first into the tunnel, dreading a return to the hole beneath, but hearing the baby's cries more clearly now. She'd pocketed the torch and when she dropped onto the table, she shone it around, shuddering as the light passed over the body of the school teacher and the child, wishing, as she had earlier, that she didn't have to leave them down here in the darkness.

The indignant shrieks of the infant, no doubt hungry and wondering why its demands were not being met, seemed to come from the opposite corner. Alex played the light around the area, seeing a twisted frame of what might once have been a door, still with sufficient strength to shore up the debris above it, making a kind of cave.

Approaching cautiously, Alex shone the torch into the depths, but although she knew she was closer to the baby because the cries were louder, she could see nothing.

'Come up, we'll widen the hole,' Azzam commanded from above.

'And bring the whole lot down?' Alex retorted, pulling carefully on a piece of broken masonry, praying the doorframe would still hold. The masonry came away, another rock, a piece of wall—slowly she widened the gap behind the doorframe until eventually she felt the softness of a person. Not the baby, the hand she grasped was too big for a baby's, and the wrist she held had no pulse.

Tears of grief and fear spilled down Alex's cheeks and deep inside her anger stirred as well. She didn't know this woman, but two children up above, and the baby if she got it out, would now be motherless. How did fate choose whom to harm? Was it just on a whim that the earth threw open a great chasm and caused this devastation?

Aware she was raging against the fates to stop

herself thinking about the possibility of not being able to rescue the infant, she set to work again, pulling out small stones, always checking, no matter how tiny her target, that moving it wouldn't cause a collapse.

The infant's cries ceased, and Alex moved more swiftly now, still careful but aware that time might make the difference between life and death, and suddenly, what she wanted most of all, was for this child to live.

She felt a small hand—even better, felt the tiny fingers move and grip her thumb. More tears flowed, but now Alex cursed them. This was no time for emotion. She had to concentrate—she had to somehow ease the baby out from beneath its mother.

Edging closer, she slid her hand along the ground, easing it beneath where she now knew the infant lay. It whimpered at the movement— was it injured? Had she hurt it?

But she *had* to get it out!

Her hand had met resistance. The baby was somehow tied to the mother. Alex closed her eyes and tried to picture the different types of slings a mother might be wearing to hold her baby close to her body.

All she could think of were the kind of things sold in baby shops at home, and this would surely be a less complicated arrangement. But whatever it was, she needed some way to cut the baby free.

Backing out of the space, she hurried to the table beneath the hole and called up to Azzam.

'I need some scissors or a sharp knife. The baby is in some kind of sling, tied to the mother, who is dead.'

Azzam heard the waver in her voice as she said the last word and wondered at Alex's strength of character that she'd even gone back down the hole in the first place, let alone be determined enough to remain and cut the baby free. He found a sheathed knife and knelt beside the hole, frustrated by again playing a secondary role in this rescue but wanting to help however he could.

'Mostly, our women tie their babies in a crisscross fashion, their scarves dangling from their necks then crossing in front and tied at the back. Can you picture that?'

'Clearly,' came the reply, 'and thanks for that. I can cut at the back of the neck and not risk stabbing the baby.'

Azzam shook his head. He'd teasingly called her wonder-woman earlier, but that's what she was proving to be. And he'd had doubts about her? He felt ashamed, not only about those doubts but about the poison he'd allowed to spread through his heart and soul, infecting his whole body not only with pain but with suspicion.

'I have the baby, I've wrapped it well—can you pull really gently?'

The woman he no longer doubted sounded exhausted and he worried that *she'd* be able to get out.

He *had* to get her out!

'Azzam?'

Once again, her voice reminded him of the immediate task.

'I'll be gentle,' he assured her. 'Tug when you're ready.'

He felt the tug and hauled slowly and steadily, the weight so slight he had to force himself not to hurry lest he injure the baby in his haste. Then suddenly it was there and he pulled the wrapping from the little face and saw wide brown eyes staring up at him and the tiny mouth open in a wail of protest.

'It's all right, little one,' he murmured, then realised he was speaking English and translated, although he was reasonably sure it was his tone of voice, not the words, that had hushed the baby.

But with the baby held against his chest he again felt that rush of longing he'd experienced earlier. Children were the future—Alex had been right. The baby *had* to be rescued.

But for now, perhaps he should be concentrating on the baby's saviour.

'Alex? Can you climb up?'

'I guess I'll have to,' she said, injecting a laugh into her voice, although he suspected she was using it to cover if not fear then definitely apprehension.

'I'm going to squirm down as far as I can so reach up and grasp my hands and I'll haul you out,' he said.

Quite how he'd manage it he wasn't sure, but he feared she might not make it on her own.

He'd sent everyone off the rubble to make the situation safer so now he set the baby down and wriggled as far as he could into the hole, forcing his shoulders between the boulders and building fragments, praying everything would hold. Two small hands grasped his, and a jolt of lightning seemed to pass right through him. He could not fail her now.

Fear for her lent him strength as he drew his knees up under his body to get some leverage. With one almighty heave he pulled her out, collapsing back onto the ground, the woman held securely in his arms, the warmth of her transferring itself to his body, his mind in turmoil as he tried to make sense of myriad reactions—relief, some anger still that she had risked so much, and—surely not—but, yes, definitely sexual attraction.

His arms tightened, and for an instant he imagined she'd snuggled into his embrace, but before he could process the thought she moved, almost abruptly, picking up the baby, and though Azzam kept a hand on her shoulder, he knew he shouldn't be holding her. Already people might be wondering why he'd held her at all, but she'd been so close to collapse, he'd had to.

'I *had* to get her out!' she whispered as she held the baby against her body. 'The mother is dead but for those two to lose a sibling as well, I couldn't bear that.'

If she was aware of Azzam's hand on her shoulder she gave no sign of it, simply rocking the baby against her chest.

'Family!' she whispered. 'Family ties are strongest, for good or ill. I *couldn't* let the baby die.'

And he wanted to hold her again. The words, he was sure, were spilling from her subconscious, but she was uttering the thoughts he'd had himself—thoughts that were ingrained in him through breeding and upbringing.

But now, looking down at her filthy, straggling hair—had she used her scarf as wrapping for the baby?—and watching as she dripped water on her little finger and held it to the infant's mouth, he wondered if it had been pain he'd heard when she'd talked of family, and what had happened to her in the past that she'd risked her life a second time to reunite the children with their sibling.

CHAPTER FIVE

REACTION to what she'd been through. That was all it was that compelled Alex to sit very still on the rubble and drip water into the baby's mouth. She was aware of Azzam squatting beside her, making her feel extremely uncomfortable about giving way to emotion against his bare chest a little earlier.

She tried to tell herself it was his fault, because the gentleness with which he'd held her after he'd hauled her out of that dark hole had broken through her reluctance to show any weakness.

Any weakness!

But the stoicism of the trapped children, the way the little girl had stayed beside her brother—these things had already cracked the protective shell she'd built around her heart and soul to prevent further damage. The man's arms had just widened the cracks and let feelings in...

'You must move from here. You are able to stand, to walk?'

Azzam would have liked to lift her in his arms and carry her and the baby to safety but she'd shied away from him earlier, thrusting her body apart from his as if being held in his arms was an affront of some kind.

Not that he'd wanted to keep holding her—well, not that he *should* have wanted to keep holding her...

She stood up and he reached out to grasp her elbow as she stumbled. She didn't pull away, allowing him to guide her to a safe area of the *wadi*, where the little girl remained, a silent sentinel beside her brother.

Azzam watched as the woman knelt beside the girl, holding the baby for her to see. He saw the questions in the child's eyes—the big question— and knelt on the other side of her.

'We will keep looking for your mother,' he said gently as the child took the baby, tucking the infant against her chest as if she was accustomed to looking after it.

Did the baby recognise its sister that a little hand reached out and grasped the girl's finger?

Azzam found he had to swallow hard and turned to find Alex had also looked away, her fingertips brushing at tears that were leaking from her silvery eyes.

She recovered first, standing up and looking around her.

'Where can I start?'

'Prioritise,' he replied. 'These high mountains mean updraughts that would make night-flying in a helicopter very dangerous. So, we won't be airlifting patients out tonight, and need to consider shelter.'

She looked bemused.

'Shelter? Is it likely to rain? Do you have heavy dew? Will it be cold?'

'No to the rain, but yes to the dew. The village headman is organising the survivors. Those able enough will continue to move rubble from the areas where it's most likely people are still trapped, particularly around the market. The children? With the teacher gone, I have arranged for some of the mothers to take them to a safe area until nightfall. There's a date palm grove a little way along the *wadi*. They will be sheltered there, away from the rubble should aftershocks occur.'

He paused, unreasonably pleased when she nodded agreement to his suggestions.

'You and I—if you feel strong enough to continue to be involved—will stay with the injured. We have some emergency packs of fluid and I've already started IV drips in five people, but I haven't examined any of the children closely. If you could examine them again, and work out what we need to keep them comfortable, I would be grateful. The headman has a generator and he is setting up lights for us to work by.'

He wondered if he should mention the leopards and for a moment regretted that he and Bahir had nagged their father into setting up the protected national park area for them and instigating a breeding programme.

No! He wouldn't mention the leopards—not yet.

Alex began with the unconscious child, again feeling all around her head for some displacement in his skull and finding, this time, a small swelling behind her ear, as if something had struck her there.

She looked up to find a man who'd been squatting a little distance away had moved closer.

'You are her father? Daddy? Papa?'

The man nodded, anxious eyes asking questions Alex couldn't understand, let alone answer. Although she could guess at their content—would she live, his daughter? Was she in pain? Why did she lie so still?

The girl had been awake earlier, she remembered, just unresponsive, but feeling the lump she realised that whatever had struck her had hit her hard enough to cause external swelling, which meant that internally her brain would have been jolted against her skull and the likelihood was that her intracranial pressure was raised. Alex thought with longing of all the tools she'd have at her disposal in a hospital to assist in a diagnosis, but this was emergency medicine at its most basic.

Azzam was setting up a children's hospital! Did it follow he was a paediatrician?

She called his name and he was beside her within seconds, kneeling to examine the little girl, feeling as Alex had felt, around the skull.

'We need to handle her carefully,' he said, and she knew he was talking to himself as much as to her, running through the protocols for head injury. 'I'll lift the head a little and we need to keep it straight to decrease pressure on the jugular veins.'

Although it was some time since she'd worked with children, Alex knew what he was thinking— the sticks she'd used to make a neck brace could be adding pressure to the blood vessels, so she unwrapped them, making a pillow out of Azzam's now-filthy gown instead.

'Slip it under her head when I lift it, then pad some of the material against her temples so she can't turn her head,' Alex told her.

The father, seeming to understand what she was doing, put his hands beside the little girl's head, holding it steady.

Azzam spoke quietly to the man, no doubt explaining the injury and what they would have to do.

'Should we intubate her to keep her airway clear?' Alex asked, her mind moving through the stages of what was little more than first aid—all that could be offered here.

'She's breathing well herself but if you can find a small face mask, we'll deliver oxygen through that.'

How could he be so calm when her fingers were shaking as she delved into the medical supplies, seeking the smallest mask she could find? She'd been in situations like this before and surely her hands hadn't shaken?

Now, consciously steadying them—thinking only of the task in hand—she fitted the mask over their patient's face, relieved to find it sealed well. Azzam had already adjusted the flow on the oxygen tank's small dial and now he secured the outflow tube to the mask, the father watching every move they made, the anxiety he was feeling evident in his anguished eyes and the tension of his body.

Thinking medically to block out all other thoughts, Alex's mind raced through different scenarios. But she wasn't alone here—she had Azzam!

'Swelling in the brain—should we restrict fluids?'

'The child needs *some* fluid,' he responded. 'Let's try thirty per cent of a maintenance dose for a start. She'd weigh, what? She's so slight. Twenty-five kilos?'

Alex understood he was asking her as a colleague, a fellow professional, and the idea steadied her, although why she'd imagined he wouldn't she had no idea.

'I'd say twenty-five kilos,' she responded, doing the sums in her head. 'You've started five drips— how much fluid do we have?'

'Enough,' he told her. 'We have to give her diuretic drugs to relieve the pressure on her brain and we can't do that without giving her some fluid. I think you'll find another bag of fluid in the kit by that tree. I'll find some mannitol in this bag and we can titrate it into the fluid.'

He paused, then said quietly, 'She'll need to be watched through the night. If the pressure builds, we might have to release it manually.'

Manually?

Alex shuddered as she stood up to fetch the fluid. Manually meant boring a hole into the child's skull, not exactly the kind of operation you wanted to carry out in the dark on a bare patch of earth that was likely to tremble any time.

Had the father understood some of the conversation that he was looking more anxious now?

This was a child—a loved child. She deserved a chance at life, so of course if they had to operate they would do it.

Alex watched as Azzam, with infinite gentleness, swabbed the little hand, found a vein, and eased a cannula into it, attached a tube, fitted the other end to the bag of fluid, calibrated it to drip in slowly and added the mannitol to filter slowly into the girl's blood.

He passed the bag to the father, picked up a hunk of masonry and spoke to the man, obviously indicating he should build a small stand for the bag, but the father shook his head and held it high, understanding what was needed but determined to do this small thing for his daughter.

'In a hospital we'd be measuring fluid output as

well,' Azzam said quietly, the rest of the sentence, *but we're not in a hospital*, left unspoken.

Alex moved on to the next child, one she hadn't found an injury on earlier, although the child had been huddled by the teacher. He'd been totally unresponsive, this little boy, and he was still limp, now held across his mother's lap, her fingers moving restlessly against his skin, smoothing his face and hair, her dark eyes filled with despair.

Alex touched the woman gently on the arm before beginning her examination, and the woman nodded to her.

The boy's stomach was distended, his pulse racing now, his breath coming in shallow gasps.

Internal bleeding?

Alex moved his mother closer to the light so she could see the child more clearly but could find no sign of bruising on his skin. She was pressing gently on his ribs when the little body went into a violent spasm and she knew he'd died, drowned in his own blood perhaps, or his heart compressed by the fluid inside him to the stage where it stopped beating.

Azzam was by her side in an instant, no doubt

having heard the woman's wail of despair. He took the little boy and laid him on the ground, his finger checking the mouth was clear of obstruction, listening for breathing, blowing two quick breaths into the child's open mouth, before his hands moved to the small chest, delivering thirty quick compressions before breathing for the boy again.

'Let me do the breathing,' Alex told him, shifting to the child's head, vaguely ashamed she hadn't acted faster, but she'd been so struck by Azzam's immediate reaction that she'd watched instead of moving.

They worked together, Alex counting the compressions out loud now, willing the little boy to live, but eventually the mother moved, taking Azzam's hand, speaking urgently to him, all but pushing him away from her son.

'She says it is the will of God,' he whispered to Alex, and she heard the despair of defeat in his voice.

Standing up, she took his hand, squeezing it as she helped him to his feet, keeping hold of it as the woman lifted her son into her arms, rocking him against her body as she swayed back and forth, moving to her harsh cries of grief.

Azzam removed his hand and walked away, and Alex could only watch him go, aware of the burden he was carrying but not knowing what to say or do to ease it.

'You did try,' was all she could offer. 'And even if we'd got him breathing again, with no facilities to operate and fix whatever was injured inside him, he would surely have died before reaching hospital.'

Azzam ignored her words, walking on to where most of the injured adults had been assembled, close by a gnarled old tree.

Alex watched him for a moment then moved on to the next child—the boy with the broken humerus. Beside him sat his sister, the baby in her arms. The baby was asleep but would surely wake hungry. How to tell the girl to take it to where the uninjured villagers were gathered so they could both get some food?

Using sign language, bringing her hands to her mouth to indicate eating, then pointing towards the palm grove, she urged the girl away, but the child had no intention of deserting her post. Alex bent and kissed her head, thinking of her own brother—Rob—whom she had loved just as devotedly, and whom she couldn't hate no matter how much he'd hurt their mother, or how much chaos he'd left behind him.

But it was *this* child she had to treat—*this* boy she had to consider! He was in shock, trembling all over, and she found the scarf she'd discarded after coming out of the hole with the baby and wrapped it around him, carefully avoiding his arm, which she'd bound against his body earlier.

'I've thirteen serious injuries, patients who, if they survive the night, will have to be airlifted out.'

Azzam had returned and his words sent shivers down her spine. Two, maybe three, people could be lifted out at a time, the helicopter flying back and forth, maybe two helicopters, but would they have the support staff, paramedics, necessary to staff two?

'So I should splint and bandage the boy's arm to hold the bone aligned until he can be taken in an ambulance?' She looked up at Azzam as she spoke.

His face was shadowed, the light behind him, but she'd heard the horror of what they were experiencing—and the death of the child—in his voice and knew that, as these were his people, he would be feeling the pain of the disaster even more deeply than she was.

'We'll only airlift out the most severely injured,' he agreed, then knelt beside her, her response to his presence gratitude that he'd returned to share the decisions that had to be made, nothing else.

Or so she told herself!

'I will help you with the boy,' he said. 'It's easier with two, and there is nothing I can do until more survivors are brought out of the rubble.'

The little girl scuttled sideways to make room for him, but now watched both adults, her gaze switching from one to the other, a pint-sized guard ready to defend her brother should they attempt to do him any harm.

'Can you tell her where to go to get some food, and if possible some milk for the baby?' Alex asked him, nodding at the child. 'Maybe do your prince thing,' she added, smiling at him, although there was little to smile about in this place of devastation.

Azzam saw the smile and felt his heart lift, the hopelessness that had been creeping on him dissolving like desert mist before the sun.

He didn't question what the woman had that could make him feel this way, just accepted the gift of optimism she'd handed him.

'Prince thing?' he queried.

'My helper by the school was most impressed by your standing, repeating your name and saying "He is the prince" in tones of absolute awe.'

'I would rather be a doctor,' he muttered at her, but he did speak to the little girl, telling her to take the baby to the date grove.

The child left, reluctantly.

'You can't be both?' Alex asked as she unwrapped the cloth—her scarf, he noticed—from around the boy's fractured arm.

'I doubt it,' he answered, although a simple 'No' would have been more truthful. 'Maybe, later on, when I know the duties expected of me and can see a path forward—maybe then I can give some time to the project of my heart.'

Project of his heart? Was it the circumstances in which they found themselves that he was telling this stranger—this female stranger—something he'd never said aloud, not even to Bahir? Oh, Bahir had known his brother was obsessive about the new hospital, but hadn't understood it was for people like these mountain folk, who feared the city and its ways, that he'd wanted to build the special hospital for children—a place where the whole family could stay beside their sick child—a place where they would not feel intimidated by machinery and uniforms and strangers tending their child.

Fortunately Alex didn't hear the phrase, or, if she did, she forbore to question it. She'd found some morphine in the kit, worked out a dose and administered it to the child while Azzam's mind had drifted far from the job in hand.

Concentrating now, he took the boy's arm, aligning the bone as best he could by feel, Alex holding the splints in place while he bound it.

She looked up at him and smiled again.

Alex—a woman he'd met less than, what, forty-eight hours ago? Yet her smile—several smiles now—had shifted his world...

The exhaustion still dogging him had caused the shift, not the smile! He had trained himself to not respond to female smiles, the hurt inside still too raw to want to trust his feelings.

Although was the hurt still there?

He tried to think when he'd last felt that stab of pain.

Maybe his lack of interest in seeking out female company lately had been more because of his immersion in his work than the fear of new heartbreak.

Heartbreak?

Did he really believe that?

Hadn't his pain been hurt pride more than anything else?

Azzam shut off the stupid thoughts racing through his head, concentrating instead on the job in hand. He finished binding the boy's arm and fashioned a sling to hold it against his chest, his mind still muddling over motives and reactions—

in all honesty, it would be easier to be considering the leopards.

'We should keep watch tonight.'

The words brought him out of his thoughts and he looked up to see the headman of the village had approached them. Welcoming the distraction, Azzam stood up to talk to him and to listen to tales of recent leopard sightings near the village and how the villagers now kept their animals inside at night to prevent attacks.

'I've been thinking about the leopards,' Azzam told him, unconsciously using not the local word, *nimr* but the English word so that Alex looked up, repeating it.

'Leopards? Leopards out here? You can't be serious? Don't leopards live in Africa? Don't they sprawl on the limbs of trees ready to drop on unsuspecting passing animals? Where are trees here?'

She sounded so indignant he had to smile.

'Arabian leopards live in the mountains—they climb rocks and cliffs to drop on their unsuspecting prey. They were close to extinction twenty years ago, but a good breeding programme means the mountain areas have been restocked with them.'

'Great!' she muttered. 'Here I was thinking that the worst thing that could happen was another earth tremor and the mountain would fall on us, but now you tell me a very large and probably hungry cat could cart me off into the night!'

Azzam found himself chuckling now, then he translated her words to the headman who also laughed, though he quickly added, 'But she is right, they'll smell blood and could prove a danger.'

'We'll set a watch. Keep everyone together, light fires if we can find fuel, and do whatever is necessary to keep the people safe. I don't want to move the injured, so perhaps we should set up camp close by where they are, although the date grove would provide better shelter.'

'We can make shelters,' the headman told him. 'We have tents for the goat and camel herders who move the animals to different pastures. We have not lost our traditional ways, not all of us.'

The man departed and before long the uninjured began to gather on the grassy area, close to where the injured lay but not too close.

Alex watched the survivors drift like shadows through the night, heard the quiet chatter as they settled around the area where she sat with the children. Some men, and possibly some women, were still removing debris and she could hear their voices, warnings sounded and sometimes cries that told of joy—another person rescued.

'Who will protect the workers on the rubble from the leopards?' she asked Azzam when he returned with the headman and began to organise the erection of temporary shelter over the area where the wounded lay.

'I will call them in shortly,' he told her. 'It is too dangerous both for them and for anyone who might still be buried underneath for people to work at night, and the generator only has so much fuel, so it's best to conserve it for emergencies.'

'And these three children—the boy and his sister and the baby? Isn't it strange no adults have come looking for them? In a village, wouldn't someone be related to them?'

Azzam frowned down at the little boy.

'Of course there should be someone who would care for them. I will ask.'

You didn't have to be a prince to be efficient, Alex thought to herself as he walked away. But did the aura of the ruler add weight to his suggestions and advice? Did him being here bring solace and comfort to people who had lost everything, including, in some cases, a loved one?

Men and women seemed to share the chores, erecting tents, finding food, lighting fires, and now the scent of the frankincense she'd first found in the shampoo perfumed the night. Was it special, as Hafa had said, because it protected the people? Or because it was from some plant native to this country?

The little girl returned, the baby in her arms and a baby's bottle, miraculously found somewhere, full of watery-looking milk. She settled beside her brother, and once again Alex's heart ached for the three children—the little that remained of the family. The child lay down beside her brother, obviously exhausted for her eyes closed and the baby slipped from her grasp.

Alex picked up the infant, awake but uncom-

plaining, and used her now-filthy scarf to tie it
to her chest. She could work among the injured
knowing the baby was secure, but she didn't want
to move too far from the children either—not
until someone had claimed them.

Azzam, too, returned.

'You should sleep, but first you must eat. I have
brought some bread. It isn't much, but with water
it will make your stomach think it's been fed.'

Once again Azzam had appeared beside her as
if teleported there, for she'd heard nothing of his
approach, but how he'd reached her paled into
insignificance against the effect the man's presence had on her. Was it the sight of the light from
the fire dancing on his bare chest that sent shivers
up her spine? Or was it nothing more than the
maleness of him, she who hadn't known a man
intimately, who hadn't even kissed a man since
David's defection? The man smell—sweat and
dust and something deeper. She probably smelt
pretty bad herself, but this smell was—

Idiot! Of course it wasn't intoxicating! She was
tired, that was all, and in a strange country with
leopards stalking the night it was only natural her

instincts would tell her subconscious to seek out a protector.

She took the bread from him and bit into it, finding it so tough she had to tug at it to free a bite. He passed the water bottle, his fingers brushing against hers, an accidental touch that caused much the same reaction as the smell of him had only minutes earlier.

'I think the little girl's ICP has decreased slightly,' she said, reminding herself she was a competent medical practitioner, not a weak and needy—and possibly slightly hysterical—female.

Azzam heard the words, but they seemed so strange, out here in the mountain pass with tumbled houses all around them and coming from a dirty, dishevelled woman standing there, a baby strapped roughly to her chest, and shapely ankles showing beneath the hem of her trousers.

'That's good,' he said, because something was obviously expected of him, but beneath the words he sensed another conversation going on. Was she afraid? Was it fear he could feel in the air between them?

She *should* be afraid! Alone in an isolated

place, in a country she didn't know, surrounded by strangers, she certainly had cause to be a little fearful if not downright terrified. Yet he didn't want to diminish the courage she'd shown earlier by saying something—by asking her if she'd like him to stay close to her, to protect her through the night.

No matter how much he'd like to do it!

'The children? Did you find out anything about them, find anyone who would take care of them now they are apparently orphaned?'

He shook off the strange thoughts he'd been having, thoughts related to being close to this woman through the night.

'It seems they are incomers, a family who arrived here a few days before the baby was born. They have been living in an abandoned cottage. The father took off within weeks of their arrival, leaving the mother and the three children.'

'And no one has befriended her?'

Even as Alex asked the question she thought of country towns back home where newcomers might be treated with suspicion but surely not totally ignored.

'Our connections are tribal,' Azzam explained, 'and although the link might be generations in the past, the people of the tribe are all related. Some tribes naturally affiliate with others, but maybe these people were…'

He paused and Alex guessed he was wondering how to explain.

'Not enemies, exactly, but from a tribe that didn't intermarry with the locals.'

'But surely children don't carry any stigma from their breeding? Wouldn't someone want to take care of them?'

'I am guessing here and will continue to ask,' Azzam told her, 'and maybe we will find someone, but you must realise these people have lost everything. To take on three extra children when you have nothing…'

He didn't need to finish. Alex nodded, thinking the villagers had probably been poor before the earthquake had struck, taking away what little they'd had. But she held the baby more tightly against her chest as her heart ached for the children no one wanted.

Azzam was talking again and she stopped

thinking ridiculous thoughts of taking the children home with her and listened.

'I must go,' Azzam said, though he didn't want to leave the woman, who looked so vulnerable as she held the baby against her chest. 'I will take a shift with the men who are patrolling. Someone has found a rifle so don't be alarmed if you hear a shot. It will probably be someone firing at shadows, but if a leopard should approach, a shot will frighten it away.'

She sank down onto the ground, one arm still held protectively against the baby.

'I'll be all right,' she assured him, but he heard the quiver of alarm in her voice and remembered the tears that had slid down her cheeks earlier.

He knelt beside her and put his arm around her shoulders, drawing her close against his body.

'You have been incredibly brave, you have done more than should be asked of any human for people you do not even know. It is all right to be afraid, even to cry, now the worst of it is over. It is also right to grieve for the ones we couldn't save.'

'The mother of the children is dead, and the

school teacher and two of the other children, too—one that I rescued and the one I left behind,' she whispered.

'But many are alive because of you,' he reminded her, feeling the softness of her in his arms, the fragility of her small bones—feeling her as a woman so once again his body stirred.

She shook her head as if denying herself the praise and the comfort of his words then shifted so they were no longer touching.

'You must go—there are things you should be doing.' Her voice was husky—tears or just exhaustion? He couldn't tell and didn't want to think about it as either would strengthen his desire to stay close to her. 'I'll be all right on my own.'

'I *must* go,' he agreed, knowing his duty lay outside this shelter, organising, making arrangements to see them all safely through the night. Yet his body was reluctant to move—the softness of the woman a temptation he hadn't felt for a long time.

Not *this* woman, his common sense warned.

He rose and left the shelter, not looking back.

Although he would have to return—he knew

that. It would be unacceptable to leave Alex and the children on their own throughout the night.

'You still intend to sleep here with the children?' Azzam asked, finding Alex much as he had left her two hours earlier, sitting by the children in the makeshift shelter.

'Of course,' she said. 'The boy is still unwell and the baby will need feeding during the night. I can't abandon them.'

Neither could he abandon her, Azzam realised. Apart from anything else, she was a guest in his country, his mother's friend. And he'd heard not fear but distinct uncertainty in her voice as she'd told him of her plans. She wasn't stupid and would realise that this tent, on the outskirts of the little tent village now set up, would be the first visited by a leopard should one come prowling, yet she'd asked nothing of him.

On the other hand...

How to explain?

'While it is understood that all people will sleep close to each other for warmth and safety, they will do so in family groups, as that is our way,' he began, aware he sounded far too tentative but unable to explain the customs that dictated this. 'The families are already settling into tents but if we share a tent, you and I, it would be...'

'Remarked on? Unseemly? Not done? There's been an earthquake, for heaven's sake. We have to do the best we can.'

He had to smile at the incredulity in her voice, especially when she added, 'Anyway, if people want to get picky, we can point out we have the children with us as chaperones.'

There was a pause, taut and expectant, before she added, 'Not that I need you to share the shelter with me. You said people will patrol the camp. I'll be quite safe.'

If she'd sounded a little less defiant—defiance hiding uncertainty—he might have let it go, but duty to this woman who was helping his countrymen insisted she be protected.

'The children would not count, neither can I leave you unprotected. I am sorry, but my position—it must seem ridiculous in your eyes, I can see that, but in this village it would be seen as...'

He turned away, battling to find the words he needed, English words that would convey the extent of dishonour him sharing a tent with her would bring, not only to his name but even more so to this woman who was innocent of anything other than a desire to help.

But there were no words—well, none he knew—in English to cover such a situation.

'It would be impossible!' He settled for simply dismissing the idea, before bringing up a solution. 'However, there *is* a way that we can do this. If you would sleep easier with my company—and I would certainly feel happier about your safety if I was with you—then we can make a marriage.'

'A marriage?' Incredulity didn't cover it—this was stark disbelief! 'We get married so you can share a tent with me? In an earthquake-stricken village wherc the choice of shelter is non-existent?'

'It is an old arrangement, usually made for the convenience of both parties but without the obligations of a real marriage. It is legal to do this, to make a *misyar* marriage for both our convenience so the people do not think that I am shaming you, or that are you a shameless...'

'Hussy is the word we'd use,' she said, actually chuckling as she said it. 'I can't believe this. It is just too weird. I know other cultures have their boundaries and it's the difference between people that makes the world the fascinating place it is, but...'

Laughter swallowed up the words and now instead of fanciful smiles in the night air, Azzam felt the stir of anger.

'Is marrying me so ridiculous?' he demanded. 'Many women would be gratified to—'

'Be proposed to by a prince?' The words were accompanied by a further gurgle of laughter. 'Oh, dear, I have to stop laughing but you must admit it's funny. Here I am, given a choice of facing a stray leopard on my own or marrying a prince, and I'm dithering over it. And on top of that there's the fact that you have this convenient kind of pseudo-marriage, which sounds to me as if it's there to cover men who might want to cheat on their wives.'

'It was not intended for that.' He sounded far

too stiff and formal, but that was because he knew it *was* used in that way from time to time. Though not to cheat, for the wife would surely know of it. 'It is also convenient for older women, widows even, who might be happy on their own but sometimes desire male company.'

He completed his explanation, his voice so cold Alex realised she'd have to stop joking about the situation, although the only way she'd been able to handle the uneasiness inside her that had followed his strange proposal had been with humour. She was wondering if she should apologise when he spoke again.

'It was intended too, for times like this, for when a woman might need the protection of a man but is without a brother or a father. If it has been made a convenience of by some people, that is by the way. For tonight and however many nights we need to remain here, would you be willing to go through with it?'

'Marriage or the leopard—it's really not a choice,' Alex said, deciding this was just one more bizarre memory she would have to take home with her. 'What do we have to do?'

'Agree, have two witnesses and the headman, who will be the local marriage official. I'll go and see him now.'

Within thirty minutes they were married, it seemed, although her husband had departed with the headman as soon as the ceremony, if it could be called that, was over. He was checking the arrangements for keeping watch, he'd said, and would talk to people about the possibility of someone taking the children into their own family.

Married so they could share a tent?

Forget that—it was nothing more than a formality. She must concentrate on what needed to be done.

Alex fed the baby, cleaned him as best she could, wrapped a bit of cloth around his nether regions then set him down, asleep, beside his sister. She wished she had something to cover them with, but all the available materials had been used.

With the siblings asleep, she moved across to the next tent where the unconscious girl lay, her father still holding the bag of fluid. The girl's pupils were still unresponsive to light and her limbs failed to react to stimuli. Despair crept into Alex's heart as she began to think this child, too, might die, but when she felt the child's fontanelle, nearly but not entirely closed, she found the small gap between the bones at the top of the skull was no longer bulging. It meant the pressure in the child's brain had decreased, and she smiled at the girl's father, hope lightening her heart.

She returned to the children—her children, as she was beginning to think of them. Azzam had left a bottle of water in the tent, and, using her bra as a washer, she wet it with a little of the precious fluid to give herself a quick wash, thankful she'd had the forethought to bring her emergency pack with the spare pair of undies in it, although she hadn't thought ahead enough to bring nappies for a baby!

The baby—he'd stir, probably wake during the night. Best he sleep next to her. But as she'd retrieved him, she'd felt the little girl's skin, had felt how cold she was, although the night was still young. She *had* to find some cover for them.

Her clothes, of course, were filthy, but the tunic top she wore came to just below her knees. She could slip off the long cotton trousers and still be as decent as a woman in a dress at home. There was enough material in the wide trousers to cover the children for the night, and in the morning, before anyone was around, she could pull them back on.

She settled down beside the children—not hers at all but three who needed someone to show care and perhaps a little love towards them. With the baby wrapped against her chest, she curled her body protectively around the siblings, resting her arm across them so they were all snuggled up together.

Azzam stood his shift on watch then walked back to where the children were, looking down at the woman in the light shed by the fire outside the tent. While he'd been gone, she'd lost her trousers, the sleeves of her tunic had fallen back and the hem of it had ruffled up, so shadows of dark and light played across her pale, slim limbs, highlighting scratches that made him angry for some reason.

Angry that she'd been hurt...

He blocked the image and the thought from

his mind, seeing the way she had placed herself between the edge of the shelter and the children. She may have been afraid of leopards but that fear hadn't blotted out her protective instincts.

He lay beside her now, adding another layer of protection for the children, but it was the warmth of *her* body that stirred him, thoughts of *her*, not the children, drifting through his mind until sleep claimed him.

CHAPTER SIX

THE baby stirred against her chest and gave a feeble whimper. Not wanting it to cry and wake Azzam or the other children, Alex slid out from between them. She unwound the scraps of material with which she'd bound the baby to her chest, found the bottle of milk, and held the teat to the infant's lips. She tried not to think where the milk—or the bottle—might have come from, and dismissed all thought of sterility from her mind.

Which wasn't that hard, as thoughts of the man who'd slept beside her were clamouring for attention.

She'd woken to the feel of his warmth and the solidity of his body, and had felt her own warmth build in response to his closeness. Not sexual warmth—or she didn't think it was—

more just a feeling of security, a sense of shared responsibilities.

He was her husband...

Nonsense, he wasn't a real husband—not in any sense. It was convenience, nothing more.

Definitely not sexual warmth!

The baby sucked avidly, reminding her of where her attention should be. Holding the bottle and baby with one hand, Alex searched through the medical supplies until she found another sling, and, padding it with cotton wool, fashioned a nappy for the infant.

'There,' she said to him as he finished the milk and snuggled against her chest, 'now you'll be more comfortable.'

She checked his sleeping siblings then tucked the baby in between them, so she wouldn't be hampered, and he wouldn't be disturbed, if she had to move to tend another patient during the night. In fact, now she was awake she should check on all the patients.

Or was she looking for an excuse to escape the man who lay, sleeping so soundly, right beside her?

An excuse to escape her thoughts?

She smiled to herself as she realised that to someone who'd battled on alone as she had recently, the warmth of shared responsibilities might be more alluring than sexual warmth.

Well, almost...

Although it had been such a long time since she'd felt any stirrings of a sensual nature, she couldn't really judge. She'd stopped feeling them long before David had opted out her of life so precipitously. When first they'd met, his insistence they not make love until they married had seemed so quaint and old-fashioned she'd admired him for it—even felt special in some way. But why had it never occurred to her to wonder why the decision didn't irk her?

Because being with David hadn't stirred her body and her senses the way this man's presence did?

Because she'd never felt much physical frustration over his decree? Maybe a quiver or two when they'd kissed, but even that had stopped long before they'd parted. In fact, in retrospect, she had to wonder if David had remained engaged to her to protect himself—to avoid a permanent commitment to another woman. Any woman!

So, if she was to feel strange stirrings now, would it be so surprising? Even in the dim light of the dying fire, the man who lay beside her was clearly something special. His face had struck her earlier, outlined against the bright whiteness of his headdress, then his body—his naked chest— so well developed.

Now the heat of him, so close…

She sat and looked at him, aware this wasn't quite right, to be studying a stranger while he slept.

Except he was her husband—didn't that excuse her?—even if he had only married her to save her name. Although he *had* made out it was equally to protect his own good standing that he'd taken the step of marrying her.

His own good standing as prince, or as a man?

She had no answer to that or to any of the questions that taunted her.

What would it be like to be truly married to

such a man? To feel his body held against hers?
To know him intimately?

Now the warmth she felt had nothing what-
soever to do with security. It burned along her
nerves, awakening responses between her thighs,
reminding her she *was* a woman and this was
what all her friends would consider a very beddable man.

A beddable man? Was she becoming addle-
brained? How could she think such a thing?

She stood up and slipped away from the sleeping children—and Azzam—moving to the next
temporary shelter where the man who had stayed
beside his daughter had attached the fluid sac to
a stout stick he'd stuck in the ground, and he now
lay sleeping, one hand on the little girl.

Alex moved quietly on, into the shelter where
the generator hummed, providing dim light for
the people caring for the wounded adults. It was
the first time Alex had seen them all lined up together, and she wondered how some of them had
survived, so severe were their injuries. A woman
moved between them, moistening lips with water,
answering cries of pain.

'I am nurse,' she said to Alex. 'I have a little English from school and university. I am doing the work of doctor in the village. Our new Highness, before he was the prince, organised health centres in all villages and I run the centre here.'

Alex nodded her understanding and was impressed by the caring way the woman worked among her patients. They were in good hands and she could return to her children, for dawn was lightening the sky and she didn't want them waking and not finding her there beside them.

Her children?

The unresponsive little girl had her father, the mother of the boy who'd died had carried her son away, and all the other children she'd rescued must be with their families. Leaving her with the three motherless ones.

Her children…

Azzam woke to the roar of an engine and the clatter of rotor blades, sounds that told him the sun was up and the helicopter had returned. He stirred and groaned as his muscles told him it was too long since he'd slept on bare earth.

He looked around, aware of an emptiness he didn't understand.

Inner emptiness?

No, that was surely hunger.

But Alex *was* gone, the baby also, although the little girl remained steadfastly by her brother's side.

'I've been foraging for food.'

Alex returned as he sat up, shaking his head to clear it of the fog that sleep had given it. Part of the fog was an image that had lingered, of this woman's slim, pale limbs, but thankfully she was now fully covered again, except for her hair, which was so dirty she was no longer recognisable as a blonde.

She had a slab of flat bread in one hand and a flask of what looked like milk. The baby, he noticed, was once again strapped against her chest. Was it instinct that she carried the baby as the local women carried their infants? Or practicality?

Probably the latter, to keep her hands free, he was deciding when she spoke again.

'I need most of this for the baby, but you need to drink something and I couldn't find any water.'

Couldn't find any water? Last night, in all the confusion, he'd heard men talking about water—about the oasis in the *wadi*—but he'd taken little notice, intent on doing what had to be done.

'There should be water,' he told her. 'It might be dirty from the debris but this is an oasis.'

She shrugged.

'Well, this is all I could find.'

He took the bread, his mind fully focussed now. Had the debris from the earthquake completely filled the oasis, or had the earthquake itself opened up the ground sufficiently for it to leak away? He'd need to set men digging further up the *wadi*—the survivors would need water, and soon.

He took a gulp of the milk—camel milk, he'd forgotten the strange taste—and ate some bread, touched the baby on the head and left the shelter before he reached out and touched Alex as well. Maybe not on the head, but on the shoulder, although every instinct told him touching her was madness.

He'd slept too soundly, that was the problem.

Now, focus on the present.

Focus on the next move.

Focus!

It sounded as if the helicopter had landed, so the most seriously wounded would have to be carried down the valley to it. So much to do, so many things to think about, but as he left Alex said his name.

'Azzam!'

He looked back at her, standing straight and tall in her dirty clothes, a baby that she didn't own strapped to her chest.

His wife, albeit a *misyar* one...

'The unconscious little girl should go on one of the helicopter trips,' she said to him, 'but can they take her father as well? I don't know for sure but it seems to me they are all that are left of their family for wouldn't the mother be here if she was alive?'

Azzam knew what she was saying and understood the father would not be separated from his daughter. Of course he would be clinging to the one remaining member of his family. Wasn't this why he, Azzam, was building the special hospital?

Yet the father would take up the space where one of the injured could be, and would add weight in an aircraft where weight had to be considered carefully.

'I will try to arrange it,' he told her.

She nodded as if understanding all the permutations of his thinking, and returned to the next shelter to examine the child once again. He watched her sign to the man before leaving the little girl and moving on to help the nurse with the adult patients, the two women tending them as best they could while they waited for their turns to be carried down the valley to the helicopter.

'That's it for today but at least all the badly injured have been airlifted out.'

Azzam appeared as night was closing in. Alex had seen him at various times during the day, although he'd spent most of his time helping carry the injured to the helicopter, remaining there with them until they were airlifted out.

Alex had stayed at the village, helping move

rubble, tending survivors who were still, miraculously, being found, and keeping an eye on the three children. As better tents, flown in by helicopter, were erected, to be used as housing until the village could be rebuilt, the local nurse tried to fit the children into other families. One woman offered to take the baby, another family was willing to care for the boy and girl, but the little girl stubbornly refused to have the family split up, remaining where she was, caring for the baby when Alex was busy elsewhere.

'There are still injured people being found beneath the rubble,' Alex reminded him, using the bottom of her tunic to wipe her face.

'The helicopter will return tomorrow and keep returning as long as it is needed,' Azzam replied. He slumped onto the ground beside where she was sitting, outside the small shelter that she thought of as 'hers'.

Theirs?

'This village is at the border of my country,' Azzam continued, tiredness making his words sound gruff and strained. 'Our neighbours in the big town further down this old trade route have been affected as well. The town is not as badly damaged but because it had a bigger population there have been more injuries. Their rescue services are at full stretch so we couldn't ask them for help, but by tomorrow evening our road to the village should be clear and we can bring in heavy machinery not only to clear the rubble but to dig a new well for the village.'

'The rescue people who've already flown in have made a difference,' Alex told him. 'They've given all the villagers a break from the digging and rubble shifting, and brought optimism as well as their strength.'

'Not to mention food and water,' Azzam said, swinging the backpack he'd been carrying onto the ground and delving into it. 'Abracadabra— isn't that what your magicians say?'

'Your magicians too, surely? Or was it "Open sesame"?'

She was more disturbed by his presence at the moment than she'd been since she'd first met him, finding herself uneasy and a little at a loss because she couldn't understand her uncertainty.

Not that he appeared to notice for he was delving into the backpack.

'Aha! Just for you!' He produced a pack of wet tissues, handing them to Alex.

'Can you manage a bath with just these?' he asked her. 'I'd have liked to ask someone to pack clean clothes for you but necessities like food and water seemed more important.'

'These will do just fine,' she managed, then, clutching the treasures to her chest, she retreated into the tent. The little girl was sitting by her brother, apparently telling him a story, the baby asleep on her knees.

'Look,' she said to the girl. Talking to the child had become a habit, although Alex knew she couldn't understand. 'Wet wipes.'

She knelt beside the children, pulled out a wipe, and wiped the boy's face, then with a clean cloth wiped the baby, finally handing three wet tissues to the little girl, who looked at them with delight before using them to scrub her face, hands and arms.

Deciding to keep the wipes for the children, Alex retreated further into the small tent, where she used the waterless cleanser from her emergency pack to wash her hands, arms and face. Then, aware of how grubby she was, she slipped off her clothes and, once again using her bra as a washer, washed the rest of her body as best she could.

Her clothes might be filthy but at least now she was kind of clean underneath. Her hair, hanging in a dirty braid down her back, didn't bear thinking about, but, deciding this was as good as it was going to get, she dressed and went back out to find that Azzam had, miracle of miracles, produced a packet of disposable nappies for the baby.

'Are you more delighted by those than by the food I'm preparing?' he asked, and she realised he was heating something in a small pot over a tiny gas stove.

'Definitely more interested in the nappies,' she told him. 'I was running out of things to use to keep him dry. As for food, I found bread and milk for the children earlier, so they're okay, but now I can smell whatever it is you're cooking there, my stomach is more than interested in the food.'

She squatted beside him and Azzam looked at her face, pale but clean, although rimmed with dirt around her hairline. A truly remarkable woman, he realised, uncaring of her own needs as she helped the strangers among whom she found herself.

Why?

She was a doctor, it was natural she should respond by helping, but surely going down that hole to rescue the children had been beyond the call of duty?

He switched his mind from the mystery of this woman to practical matters.

'When all the injured have been airlifted out, we will be able to leave, probably some time tomorrow,' he told her. 'A paramedic will come in on the first flight in the morning and he and the nurse should be able to cope with the less severely injured, who are staying here. Most of the personnel we'll fly in next will be people to continue digging and others to get services set up so the village can function while it's rebuilt.'

'And the children?' she asked, nodding her head towards the inside of the tent.

The children? He found himself frowning at her question.

'I thought the headman was arranging for other villagers to take them.'

'The boy is feverish, probably with an infection, and the girl won't leave him, or the baby, and no one in the village can manage all three.' She hesitated, then frowned as she asked, 'Do you know what has happened to the father? I know you said they were from a different tribe but there's something more. The nurse couldn't explain when I asked her, but it seems to me as if these children are—well, some kind of outcasts? Could that be? Does that happen? Could their father have done something bad? And if so, would that mean that if the children remain here, they might not be treated as kindly as they should be?'

'I will ask,' Azzam told her, 'but for now forget the children and eat.'

He tipped half the rations into a bowl and handed it to her, offering a plastic spoon he'd scavenged from the helicopter, thinking she'd find it easier than using flat bread to scoop up food.

'I wouldn't like to think they'd be unhappy—

unhappier than they must already be with the loss of their mother. And it seems strange that they are so alone when your mother said it was a long-held tradition to welcome others to the camp. So there must be some definite reason they *weren't* welcome.'

He turned towards her.

'Are you always this persistent?'

She smiled and once again he felt something move inside him, although he knew it couldn't be attraction.

Gratitude, perhaps, that she'd done so much for his people.

'Only when it concerns the welfare of small children,' she said, 'and possibly patients who aren't very good at standing up for themselves.'

'And elderly women who are against a management plan for their asthma,' he added. 'I read the way you worded my mother's plan, making it simple for her yet emphasising the importance of prevention rather than cure. I know she is unwilling to take drugs unless it's absolutely necessary. That is why you were concerned for her?'

She glanced up from her meal but as night had

fallen and he'd turned off the stove he couldn't read the expression on her face.

'I liked her,' she said, and he believed her, though it brought into his mind once again the disparity that kept niggling at him about this woman. Here he saw unselfishness of spirit as she gave generously of herself in the devastated village, so why did he still see the faint shadow of Clarice behind her, the shadow of a woman who'd come to his country to get as much as she could out of it?

He knew, instinctively, that Alex was different, so why couldn't he get Clarice out of his mind?

And suddenly it came to him—the answer so simple he could have laughed out loud. The betrayal he'd felt hadn't been heartbreak at all—pique maybe but nothing irretrievable. His pain had come from the physical side of things, from the fact that Clarice had been able, without a second's hesitation, to go from his bed to Bahir's. That, to him, who had believed in fidelity, had been the ultimate betrayal.

He was shaking his head at the fact that he'd let it poison his life for so long, all because he hadn't seen his own reaction clearly, when Alex's voice recalled him to where he was.

'That meal was delicious,' she said, setting down the empty bowl. 'Thank you.'

Then she chuckled, a warm, rich sound that seemed to fill the night with smiles.

'A meal cooked by a prince,' she teased. 'Not everyone can boast of such a thing.'

But the laughter didn't linger, her voice serious as she added, 'You haven't answered me about the children. I wouldn't like to leave here not knowing what will happen to them.'

'Arrangements will be made,' he said, speaking firmly so the subject could be dropped and he could go back to considering where such a fancy as a night filling with smiles could have come from. He was a practical man, always had been. Bahir, now, he might have thought such a thing, for at heart he'd always been a romantic dreamer. Yes, his brother was still with him—just a little...

Alex moved, standing up, thanking him again for the meal and the things he'd brought, saying good night...

More unsettled than ever by Azzam's presence, Alex escaped into the tent. He would stand a watch, surely, and she could be asleep before he came in to sleep, and if that was regret she was feeling, she needed her head read!

Proximity, that's all it was, and being alone in a strange place—of course she'd feel drawn to a man who wanted only to protect her.

Protect her body *and* her reputation, she thought, smiling to herself, although the nurse had told her of leopard sightings during the previous night and protection of her body wasn't such a joke.

Yet, remembering how it had felt the previous night, the warmth she'd drawn from his body, she felt a shiver of apprehension, admitting to herself how easy it would be for his body to seduce hers.

Not that he'd have the slightest interest in her that way, which made her reactions even more shaming.

Except that humans were designed that way for the continuation of the species. Without attraction between men and women, the race would have died out centuries ago.

Having thus excused herself for her wayward thoughts and feelings, she lay down, curled around the children, her arm across them once again.

The children!

Thinking about them would take her mind off her other wandering thoughts.

If she was married, could she adopt the children?

Though how could she work the hours she did and bring up a family?

If Azzam would agree, perhaps, to provide enough money to keep the children, she could take them home with her. No, it wouldn't work. Bad enough for them to lose their parents, but to lose their country? How could she consider bringing them up in a strange land, she who didn't even understand them when they spoke?

Her arm brushed against the lamp she'd found earlier in the rubble, a beautifully shaped brass lamp that the little girl had claimed as hers.

Now it reminded Alex once again of the fairytales that kept recurring to her throughout this whole adventure and she had to wonder whether, if she rubbed the lamp, a genie might appear. A fantasy, of course, but there was no harm in dreaming. She could ask the genie for a home for all of them. A second wish would be for money—not a lot, just enough to cover the debt—and she'd keep the third for when it might be needed. With Rob's debt paid, she could stay here, in this strange and fascinating land, and bring up the children with their friends...

She chuckled as she held the lamp, laughing at herself because she couldn't bring herself to rub it. The whole experience she was going through was so unbelievable a genie *might* just appear.

'You are laughing again? Surely not still at our marriage?'

Azzam had entered the tent as silently as he always appeared, and she rolled over and looked at the dark shadow that was him, hunkered on the floor beside her.

'No, now I'm laughing at my own silly fancies,' she said. 'Working out what three wishes I would ask for should a genie emerge when I polish my Aladdin lamp.'

She passed the little lamp to him, and Azzam ran his hands over it, wanting to ask what she would wish for but already too confused about this woman to be hearing of her wishes for the future.

The less he knew of her the better. He'd decided that while walking the perimeter of the camp with the headman. Already he knew he'd have a problem with the children who were, he'd discovered, not exactly outcasts but from a family held in disrepute by their own tribe and therefore not likely to be exactly welcome in a family here.

He'd have to take them home with him. There were plenty of staff to care for them and they would give his mother a new interest. His family had a tradition of taking in lost or orphaned children running right back through the centuries, and his mother would take a personal interest in them.

Yet as he sat down on the rock-hard earth and felt the proximity of the woman who was now his wife, he wanted more than anything to know her wishes, and to hear her talk and laugh again. Well, maybe not more than anything, because somewhere deep inside a desire to hold her was also building up within him, and if that wasn't stupidity, he didn't know what was.

He went for the easy option.

'What would you wish for?'

'You can't tell wishes,' she told him, her voice, and her face as far as he could tell in the dim light, deadly serious. 'Otherwise they don't come true.'

And now the urge to hold her had changed to an urge to give her a hug, for the words had had a wistful quality about them, and this strong woman who'd crawled into a dark crevice to rescue children, and who had worked with the men shifting rubble, sounded...vulnerable!

'Money can make most wishes come true,' he pointed out.

She shook her head.

'I've never had enough to know if you're right or wrong, but while I agree it could help—that it could make some things easier in a person's life—I wonder if it's true, generally speaking? Can it buy happiness, for instance? Can a designer handbag or a brilliant diamond bring true happiness? And can money guarantee the people you love won't die?'

As soon as the words were out of her mouth, Alex regretted them. She turned to Azzam and rested her hand on his arm.

'I'm sorry, that was a totally insensitive thing to say. You must miss your brother terribly.'

He was looking away from her, but she felt him move, and he put one hand over hers where it lay on his arm, holding it there.

'Will you sit with me outside for a short time? The stars are out and everyone should see a night sky in the desert.'

Sit under the stars with him?

Let starlight work its magic when she suspected she was already on the way to being in love with this man?

Of course she couldn't!

'Please?' he added, and she knew she would. She stood up and walked in front of him, stopping just beyond the door to their shelter and looking up at the magic of a billion bright stars in a black-velvet sky.

He took her hand and led her to a smooth rock

not far from the tent, then used gentle pressure on her hand to ease her down beside him. Her hand felt safe in his.

How peculiar!

When had hands felt unsafe?

And was her mind wandering down this obscure alley so she wouldn't think about the profile she could now see clearly in the bright starlight? The clean, strong profile that would be etched forever in her mind?

'I felt such anger at first,' he said, speaking so quietly she had to strain to hear the words, but even straining it was hard to miss the pain behind them. 'It was such a useless waste of life—and of a life that had so much to offer. Anger blotted out the grief, and now the situation—not the earthquake but being thrown into a role I wasn't trained for, and certainly never wanted—that has takcn all my attention.'

Alex squeezed the fingers of the hand that still clasped hers.

'Grief will come when you are ready for it,' she said quietly. 'I know this for a fact. Some people find it there immediately, and find release in it, but others need to get through that fog of disbelief—and anger too, that's a legitimate reaction—that follows sudden death before they can remember the person they loved and truly grieve their loss.'

He moved the hand that had held hers imprisoned, freeing her fingers.

Was she sitting too close?

Had her words been too personal?

He didn't shift away, or remonstrate, instead using his freed hand to touch her cheek, turning her head towards him in order to drop the lightest of kisses on her lips.

'My good wife,' he whispered, as he drew his head back just a little. 'Offering comfort and wisdom to your husband.'

Alex was still coming to terms with the kiss, attempting to still the commotion in both her brain and her body, when he added the compliment—and with it added to the commotion...

'I'm not a real wife, remember,' she said lightly, hoping to relieve the tension in the air around them.

'You're very real to me,' he said, then he pointed to the stars, naming the constellations they could see, different names from the ones Alex knew, although apart from the Southern Cross she'd never been able to identify stars.

'This is Alchibah,' he said, pointing upwards where she strained to pick out one particular star from all the others. 'His name means tent, and over there, beyond that bright constellation, is Adhara, the maiden. So I am sitting here, outside the tent, with Adhara, the maiden. How fortunate can a man be?'

He slid one arm around her shoulders and held her close as they both continued to gaze in awe at the magic of the night sky, but the warmth Alex felt, being held so casually, was out of all proportion to the situation. Somehow, the words, and being pressed against his side, had raised a firestorm of reactions in her body—rapid heartbeat, heat racing along her nerves and a heaviness in her blood that made her want to let go of all her cares and, just for a while, experience nothing but feeling and emotion.

Could he feel it? Did it have to be two-sided, this intense attraction that stroked against her skin, even brushed her breasts, making her nipples tingle? But she didn't want to move, for to do so might spoil the moment, might break the web of sensation his body was spinning so effortlessly around her.

She *had* to move!

She *had* to rub her hand across her chest to stop the ache that started there and zeroed down between her thighs.

'You feel it too?' he murmured, then he was kissing her, kissing her properly. 'Is it nothing more than the magic of the night, do you think?' he continued murmuring against her lips, 'or something very special that involves just the two of us?'

She answered by initiating the next kiss, and when she drew away to catch her breath found herself admitting ignorance.

'I've no idea,' she told him honestly, revelling in the arms that held her firmly against his chest, revelling in the feel of his hard body against hers. 'It probably is the night—moon magic or starstrike, perhaps—because it's nothing I've ever felt before.'

She'd offered him a gift with that confession, Azzam realised. A gift he would hold close to his heart.

But it was a gift that prevented him from taking this attraction further—not here and now anyway. Yes, she was ripe for seduction, he could feel desire thrumming in her body, but would it not be a betrayal of her innocent admission, to take advantage of her? And what of later—back in the real world—what of the consequences of such an action?

Having finally sorted out the reasons the pain of Clarice's defection had lingered so long, he knew he couldn't go into an affair with this woman lightly. It was something he needed to think clearly about, and his mind, right now, was beyond clear thinking.

He kissed her once again, but gently this time, and equally gently disengaged himself from her.

She looked at him, questions in her eyes, then must have read something in his face that made

her offer him a rueful smile and a little nod
before she rose to her feet and went inside their
little shelter.

CHAPTER SEVEN

THEY flew back to the palace at about midday, Alex, Azzam and the three children the only passengers in the helicopter.

After a relatively sleepless night—he shouldn't have kissed her or mentioned the attraction, he shouldn't have seen her face by moonlight, the pale, ethereal beauty of her remaining in his head to haunt his dreams, he shouldn't have unburdened himself to her or talked about the stars or held her close—Azzam was happy to be returning home.

Until the helicopter landed and he stepped out to realise Clarice was there to meet them. For all her earlier protests that she was too distraught to handle her duties as the ruler's widow, mourning had obviously passed her by. The traditional white that was the colour of mourning had been set aside and she was dressed in the bold, vivid blue she knew set off her eyes, her skin and her hair tones, the tunic and the bottom of her loose trousers elaborately bejewelled so she dazzled in the sunlight.

The draught from the rotors had blown the head-scarf—something she'd never secured too well—back from her golden locks, so she came hurrying towards him, all bright and golden, crying out his name.

'I have been so worried for you,' she said, ignoring the staff gathered there *and* the other passengers and flinging her arms around him. 'Had anything happened to you on top of Bahir's death, I would have had to die myself.'

Her lush body pressed against him and for a moment he was a young man once again, meeting this golden beauty for the first time. She had dazzled him then in a way he'd never felt before and he'd fallen headlong into love, only to discover, once she met Bahir, that he, Azzam, was not the man for her.

The chatter of the children as they disembarked reminded him of where he was, and he turned to see Alex carrying the baby and herding the boy and girl away from the rotors of the aircraft. He eased away from Clarice, suspicious now of this unexpected welcome. Clarice, he had long since learned, always had an ulterior motive.

He reached out to Alex, took her hand, and drew her forward, aware that what he was about to do was wrong, yet unable to resist. He told himself it wasn't payback for that long-ago rebuff, and in truth it wasn't. This was instinctive, preparation for something that lay ahead, although he wasn't quite sure what.

'Clarice, this is Alex, my wife.'

Alex stared at the vision of golden beauty in front of her, frozen in place by the words Azzam had uttered. She realised this was some kind of ploy, one she didn't understand, and anger at being used this way began to grow inside her.

'I need to get the children inside, to bath and feed them and find a bedroom for them,' she said to Azzam, removing her hand from his grasp. 'Then I must get the boy to a hospital so his arm can be x-rayed.'

'I will organise it,' he said quickly, perhaps registering, even regretting, that he'd upset her.

'I will find a woman who will care for them. As for the boy, I shall take him myself. If the break is well aligned, we can put a cast straight on it.'

The woman, Clarice, made a protesting noise, but Alex's problem was with the man, not her.

'The boy is injured,' Azzam told Clarice, then he turned again to Alex.

'I will find someone also, to help you. You, too, need food.'

'Not to mention a bath!' she snapped, disturbed in ways she didn't understand by the tension she could feel in the air.

Who *was* this woman?

His girlfriend?

And if so, why aggravate her by introducing his 'wife' when she, Alex, wasn't a real wife at all?

Clarice?

Had she heard the name before?

She was far too tired to think right now, and getting the children bathed and fed was a priority. Several servants had appeared, Azzam rattled off some orders, and one young girl came forward, talking gently to the children, another stepping forward to take the baby from Alex.

'No, I'll take him. Just lead me back to my room,' Alex said, remembering this young girl as one she'd seen helping serve at dinner with Samarah about a hundred years ago. Could it only have been three days?

She followed the two young women and the children from the helicopter pad into a rear entrance to the palace, then along a familiar corridor to her room, where Hafa was waiting for her.

'We had word from the helicopter that the children were coming,' she said. 'The room next to yours is prepared for them and Ghaada, who loves all children, will be looking after them. I will help her bath and clothe and feed them, and His Highness will take the boy for X-rays, leaving you free to have a bath yourself.'

Brooking no argument, Hafa took the baby from Alex's arms and went with the children to the room next door, now talking in their language and waving her free arm, apparently assuring the little girl that Alex would be nearby.

Another young servant was waiting in Alex's

bedroom, and to Alex's delight she, too, spoke English.

'I will help you,' she said simply, then she moved forward and as Alex raised her arms, the woman drew the filthy tunic over her head. Then she released the band around the plait and teased out Alex's hair, murmuring at the state of it.

'I have run a bath for you,' she said, ushering Alex into the bathroom, where there was a foaming tub with the scent she now knew so well rising from the bubbles with the steam.

Stripping off the rest of her clothes, Alex stepped into it, lying back in the warm water and feeling fatigue, as well as grime, ease from her body.

The young woman had followed her, and now she proceeded to wash Alex's hair, ignoring Alex's feeble protest that she could manage. Instead, she gave herself up to the luxury of it, and lay there, relishing the woman's fingers massaging her scalp—relishing the simple pleasure of being clean.

She eventually emerged from the bath and had a quick shower as well, washing off the grime she was sure would have lingered in the bath water.

As she stepped out, the young woman wrapped her in a thick, warm towel, patting her dry.

'Enough!' Alex finally told her. 'I can look after myself now, but thank you anyway.'

'No, I am to see you eat and rest,' she said, polite but stubborn. She held out a white towelling robe for Alex to put on then led her to a table by the window in the huge bedroom. An array of food was laid out there, with jugs of fruit juices and pots of coffee as well. Suddenly aware of her hunger, Alex sat down at the table and began to pick at what was on offer—sliced fruit, flat bread, meat and cheeses of different kinds, all things chosen to tempt a very tired woman's appetite.

Once fed, she realised sleep had become a priority, and she explained to the girl that she really needed a short rest. The short rest became three hours, and she woke with a start, unable to believe she could have slept so long and so deeply.

'Where are the children? Are they all right? The boy, how is his arm?'

Hafa had returned and must have been watching over Alex as she slept, for she came forward, assuring her all was well and that the older children had been playing in the garden once the boy's arm had been set.

Now she waved her hand towards the dressing room.

'When you are dressed, I will fix your hair,' she said. 'His Highness wishes you to bring the children to his mother in half an hour. We do not have much time.'

Alex found herself smiling for the first time since her return to the palace.

'I'm a doctor,' she said. 'I can be dressed and ready to move in two minutes. Half an hour is a luxury.'

Hafa returned her smile.

'But today you need not hurry like that,' she said, leading Alex, still clad in the cotton robe, across the dressing room and opening the doors to reveal that Alex's meagre wardrobe had been supplemented by at least another dozen outfits, far more exotic looking than the plain tunics and trousers that had been there originally.

Before Alex could protest the children returned, the boy and girl now dressed in pristine white clothing, the baby swaddled in a soft white muslin cloth. The little girl, Tasnim, Alex remembered, stared in awe at the clothes in the closet then pointed to a pale, silvery tunic and trouser set, pointing next at Alex.

Laughing at the child's delight, Alex stooped and hugged her, then turned to Hafa.

'I know she is Tasnim, but could you find out the other children's names, and tell her mine is Alex? I have tried with sign language but we both get muddled.'

Excited conversation followed and in the end Alex knew the boy was Zahid, the baby Masun.

Ghaada removed the children, promising to wait in the colonnade just outside the door until Alex was ready to take them to meet Samarah. Alex dressed in the outfit Tasnim had chosen, although she felt self-conscious about donning such beautiful clothes. The material was the finest silk, the palest blue-green colour shot through with silver. She had no make-up, but Hafa produced a box of lipsticks and a beauty case of unused cosmetics.

Shaking her head at such unimaginable luxury—that a guest room should come complete with new, expensive cosmetics—Alex chose a pale pink lipstick and used that on her lips before brushing her hair, tugging at the tangles, then covering it with a scarf that matched her outfit.

'I'm done,' she said to Hafa, who looked concerned that anyone could pay so little attention to her toilet, but Alex waved away the protest she began to make, saying, 'Samarah wishes to meet the children. She already knows me, although she might not recognise me in these beautiful clothes.'

She came towards them like a silvery ghost, carrying the baby and herding the two little ones in front of her. Azzam knew he was staring, but he couldn't stop himself. He, who'd always thought golden beauty unsurpassable, was now struck dumb by this delicate, silver wraith.

'You have brought me children to love,' his mother cried, holding out her arms and speaking now to the two little ones in their own language. They came to her, as children always did, and she held them close then looked up at Alex, standing there with the baby.

'You will let me hold him too?' she asked, and

Alex passed the white bundle to Samarah then knelt to put her arms around the children as well, so all three of the orphans were enclosed in the loving embrace of the two women.

The scene was burning into Azzam's eyes, like a painting seen and never forgotten, when he realised Clarice was speaking to him—Clarice, who had never been far from his side since his return, objecting when he turned her away from his own quarters so he could wash and dress.

'I have been thinking about Bahir,' she was saying, and Azzam had just restrained himself from demanding to know what else she should be thinking about so soon after his death, when she continued.

'And what he might wish for me.'

Ah, that was more like the Clarice he'd come to know. She was concerned about herself, not about her dead husband—concerned about her place in things now.

'He would not wish for me to be sad and lonely,' Clarice continued. 'You, his brother, must know that's true.'

Unfortunately, Azzam did. Bahir had been

so besotted he'd have given Clarice the world,
had it been at his disposal. He'd certainly lav-
ished her with riches—palatial homes back in
the U.S., which she visited regularly, a ski lodge
in Switzerland, an apartment in London, not to
mention jewellery worth more than the GDP of
many small countries. She was hardly going to
be cast out into the world as a poverty-stricken
widow.

Yet she was after something more. He knew
her well enough for that to be more than a
suspicion.

'*Are* you sad and lonely?' he asked.

'Of course I am,' she snapped. 'That's why
we're talking. I think we should be married. It is
within the bounds of propriety in your country
for a man to marry his brother's widow, I've read
about it.'

A rage he'd never felt before rose up in
Azzam.

'How can you be thinking of marriage to another man when my brother has been dead little
more than a week? How does your mind work
that you are putting this pressure on me? Have

you no feelings? No propriety? No sense of right or wrong?'

She turned to face him, the beautiful golden hair lit from behind by the sun so she seemed to gleam with light, her perfect features beautifully made up, her blue eyes shining at him. And as he watched she slid the tip of her tongue along her lower lip, wetting it so it, too, shone.

It was a gesture she'd used on him many years ago and now he wanted to turn away from her—to never see that face again.

'You would have married me all those years ago had Bahir not come along,' she reminded him, making him feel ashamed at the truth she spoke.

'I cannot think of this now, let alone talk of it. It is beyond anything anyone could imagine, that you would talk of marriage now. Bahir is barely dead. At least respect the rules of mourning if you're throwing rules at me.'

'Three months and eleven days?' She all but shrieked the words at him. 'You expect me to be without a man for all that time?'

The crudity of it, on top of the lack of respect

she was showing his brother, angered Azzam so much he had to turn away from her lest he say something he would later regret.

'We will talk again,' he managed to say, through teeth clenched tight to keep in words that would do more harm than good.

'Soon!' she retorted, and he heard a threat in the words.

He spun towards his own quarters, knowing she wouldn't follow him there, then remembered he'd left Alex with his mother, and in a kind of limbo, for she'd be uncertain what her role was now, and would no doubt be thinking of returning to her home.

A stab of something he hoped was only regret slashed through him, but what would hold her here?

The children?

For a while—until they were settled in the palace. He thought he knew her well enough now to understand she wouldn't just walk away because they had shelter, food and clothing. She was the adult they'd clung to after losing their mother—she would understand that.

He returned to the open part of the wide colonnade where it was the habit of the women to gather every afternoon. Alex was seated on carpets by his mother's knee, the little boy this time on her lap, while the little girl, Tasnim, chatted to his mother, who still held the baby in her arms.

The thought of marrying Clarice had made him feel nauseous, while the sight of Alex by his mother's knee had him feeling very different—and unlikely—things.

Bahir, I need you!

The inner cry went up, so heartfelt he could feel it rip right out of his chest, but Bahir was gone and he had to solve the riddles on his own. It was his job to make decisions, not only for the country but for this family...

Alex listened as Samarah and one of her aides, Afifa, translated snippets of Tasnim's conversation. She felt strangely at ease—peaceful—here at Samarah's knee, Zahid dozing on her lap, listening to the chatter of the women and the wondering questions of Tasnim.

It was nothing more than a reaction to the

last few days, she understood that. The tension she'd kept hidden beneath the surface as she'd helped the earthquake survivors was now gone, and in its place not emptiness, just a feeling of contentment.

Which would, she knew as she watched Azzam return from his assignation with the beautiful Clarice in the garden, soon be over, for once the children were settled, she would return to Australia and this little interlude would be as much a fairy story as Aladdin and his magic lamp.

'You will stay while they become used to life here?'

Alex smiled up at Samarah.

'I was thinking that just now. I shouldn't stay. There are reasons why I should return to work at home but, yes, I won't leave the children until I know they feel comfortable in their new surroundings.'

Samarah reached out and Alex felt her light touch, like a blessing, on her head.

'You work too hard. I knew that when I met you, though you always pretended it was nothing to be visiting me outside your working hours. You were too tired, too thin, too worn down by work. There is a reason?'

Alex looked at the woman she had grown to admire, and knew she couldn't lie.

'There was—is, in fact—a reason, but it's personal, Samarah. Just something I must do.'

It sounded feeble so she added something she knew Samarah would understand.

'A family thing.'

Samarah studied her for a moment then nodded, as if accepting that to question Alex further would be rude.

'But while you are here,' Samarah continued, 'you must see more of my country than a few rooms in the palace and a destroyed village. A car shall pick you up in the morning. Take the older children with you, for they, too, will enjoy the sights. Hafa will accompany you, and Ghaada will mind the baby.'

'It is I who should be showing you around.'

Alex looked up at the sound of Azzam's voice, and realised that, as ever, he'd rejoined the group in that silent manner he had, so quietly she hadn't heard him come.

'Of course you can't take time to do that.' Clarice must have been right behind him, for the words, cold and dismissive, spun through the air. 'You've already been neglecting your duties, Azzam. Some things can't stop because Bahir is dead. Trade delegations, important politicians visiting from overseas, your own business people—your days will be too full to be taking children and their nanny on a guided tour.'

Alex looked from one to the other. Clarice was probably right, but from what she, Alex, knew of Azzam, he wasn't a man to take orders from anyone.

She knew she'd guessed right when he came to sit beside her.

'Their nanny, as you call her, is my wife,' he said, the coldness in his voice cracking in the air like ice crystals. 'And after what she has done for my country and my people—*my* people, Clarice—I should be spending my life trying to repay her.'

This was entirely too creepy to be true, Alex

decided, processing the words but guessing they were being said for a reason beyond the charming compliment embedded in them. The problem was that it was hard for her to work out what was going on when the bits of her that were touching Azzam, so close she couldn't avoid contact, were feeling drawn towards him, as if wanting to cuddle into him, for heaven's sake!

Why was he talking this way? As if he owed her—worse, as if he cared...

Clarice had thrown one look of fury in Alex's direction then stalked away, and suddenly Alex understood. It was a little play for Clarice's benefit.

To make her jealous?

Though why would she be jealous of any woman in her brother-in-law's life? What was Azzam to her apart from her husband's brother?

And worst of all, did Azzam think so little of her, Alex, that he would use her as a weapon against this woman?

The thought killed the treacherous warmth as suspicion wormed its way into her heart.

'She has different ways of showing grief so we

must forgive her,' Samarah was saying, and Alex knew she was trying to ease a situation that had grown suddenly tense, for all the women were now looking from the departing Clarice to Azzam, as if asking themselves the same questions Alex had pondered.

'Grief is no excuse for rudeness, Mama,' Azzam said, though he softened the words by adding, 'although I think you would excuse the devil himself, you are so soft-hearted.'

Silence fell on them, not an uncomfortable silence now but one in which Alex's awareness of Azzam had time to grow again, so, in spite of the reservations she was now feeling about this man, her nerves twitched and twittered at each other and sent wayward messages to her brain.

'Unfortunately she is right.' Azzam broke the quiet. 'I do have duties that will prevent me showing you my country, but tonight I'm free. No one has expectations of me tonight. Will you trust the children to Ghaada and Hafa and have dinner with me?'

What could she say? Samarah and the other women were all urging her to agree, and the wild chatter that followed their English words made her think they were suggesting places he should take her.

'Let Azzam plan his own adventure—he's a grown man,' Samarah said calmly. 'But you, child—' she touched Alex on the head again '—wear the silvery gown you will find in your dressing room. I was right in thinking the pale colours would look much better on you than the dark ones you chose for practicality rather than beauty.'

'*You* chose those clothes for me?' Alex asked her. 'Thank you, but there are far too many, and they are way too fancy.'

'Hush,' Samarah said. 'After what you have done for our people, we should be giving you a palace, not just a few articles of clothing. As for the gown, you can wear a cloak over it if you feel it too bare to wear in public, but somehow I think Azzam has a private tour in mind.'

Azzam stirred beside her, while Alex puzzled over the words. She turned to him, but his face revealed nothing, the strong lines giving no hint of what might lie ahead.

Until he smiled and said, very quietly so only she could hear, 'If the silver gown makes you look more beautiful than the outfit you are wearing, it might be best you wear the cloak over it and we go to *very* public places.'

Was it really a compliment? Did he mean it? Alex looked around, thinking Clarice might have returned to within earshot, but Bahir's widow was nowhere in sight.

Which didn't stop Alex feeling distinctly uncomfortable. How long had it been since anyone had paid her a compliment? Well, sometimes someone at work might remark on a job well done, but a compliment on her looks? And coming from a man who was surrounded by beautiful women?

Suspicion returned, but excitement had sneaked in as well. She hugged Zahid and set him on his feet, watching as he went into the garden to explore with Tasnim, his wounded arm held securely in a sling.

Tonight, she, Alex, would forget all the confusing questions her brain kept throwing at her, and behave as if she'd rubbed her lamp and wished for just one magical night. She'd wear the silver gown, and the high-heeled silver sandals she'd spotted in the wardrobe.

She'd dance with the prince and have the wondrous memory of it all to take home, tucked into her heart. And when work and the life she'd chosen got too much for her, she could take it out and marvel at it, remembering...

'You are rubbing your lamp and wishing again,' Azzam said softly. 'I can tell from your smile.'

Now she smiled directly at him.

'Actually, I'd shifted from the magic lamp to one of our European fairy tales. I was thinking I'd be like Cinderella going to the ball. Do you know the story?'

He grinned at her.

'Can you imagine a father in my culture allowing his boys to be brought up on fairy stories? Oh, my mother told Bahir and I the stories of our land, but fairy stories from another land? I have heard of this Cinderella but I don't know the story. Perhaps later you will tell me.'

Alex needed only an instant to realise that it wasn't a story she would wish to tell this man—

particularly not the bit about Cinderella getting to marry the prince.

'Or we can talk of real life perhaps,' she said, and heard a faint whispering sigh as if a dream had just floated out of reach.

CHAPTER EIGHT

HAFA helped her dress, as excited as if it was she, not Alex, going out to dinner with the prince. She brushed Alex's fine hair until it shone, then plaited two strands of it, one from each side of her parting, linking them behind her head with a silver ribbon.

'Not only will they keep your hair from trailing in your dinner,' she joked when she pushed Alex in front of the mirror to admire her work, 'but they make you look like a princess.'

'Which I'm not,' Alex told her, but Hafa shook her head.

'Of course you are. It is all over the palace that His Highness introduced you as his wife.'

Alex smiled at Hafa's innocent acceptance of what had played out in the colonnade.

'Our *marriage* was to protect both my and his reputation. It wasn't real.'

She didn't add that he'd brought it up—made it public—for some reason of his own, neither did she add her suspicions of this reason. She couldn't work out why, but she was certain it had something to do with his sister-in-law, because if looks could kill, Alex would be dead and buried by now.

She was still thinking about this, while Hafa fussed over the dress, when a young girl came to tell her Azzam was waiting. The girl led Alex out the back way—the way she'd gone to find the helicopter, and to her surprise it was a helicopter awaiting her. Not the big one, which was probably based at the hospital now, still involved in missions to the ruined village, but a small one, like a monster dragon fly, painted in what she now recognised as the royal colours of black, white and silver.

Apprehension shafted through Alex's body—this was too much, she couldn't do it, she couldn't go flying off into the night in a glamorous silver dress with this man she barely knew. This *wasn't* a fairy story and this kind of thing didn't happen to ordinary, everyday Alexandra Conroy.

Something very like panic built in her head, swirling there, while something that definitely wasn't apprehension slithered along her nerves, and the feelings she'd been beginning to suspect she had for this man made her body tingle with awareness.

'Not a carriage made from a pumpkin, my lady, but the best I could do,' Azzam said, although he'd had to force the words out through a very dry throat, so beautiful did Alex look.

The silvery eyes flashed suspicion. This was not a woman you could win with sweet words or easy compliments.

'I thought you didn't know about Cinderella,' she said, obviously not as impressed by him in his best gown with the silver braid down the front as he'd been by her in the silver gown.

He offered a smile that he hoped looked genuine, although from the inside it felt strained and tight. He, who was normally relaxed with women, was suddenly tense and uneasy in ways he didn't understand.

'I looked her up on the internet,' he said. 'As

you seem to know of our Aladdin, I thought I should know of her.'

At least that had her smiling! He took her hand to lead her to the aircraft, helping her into the passenger seat, touching her with hands that felt hot and clumsy.

'We are not going far and this little beauty is not very noisy so you won't need the communication helmet.'

Even more dry mouthed now, he tucked the silver dress around her legs so it wouldn't get caught in the door, and felt the warmth of her flesh beneath the fine material. He should stop right now. This was madness. He could invent an urgent phone call, pretend a text message had come into his cellphone as he walked around the helicopter to take his seat…

Except he'd deliberately not brought his cellphone with him, wanting to give this woman one special night to remember of Al Janeen before she disappeared out of his life.

Or was he hoping for something more?

Hoping she might fall in love with his country and maybe not disappear?

Fall in love with *him*?

He was aware this was the height of stupidity because she hadn't given the slightest indication that she was interested in him, so he had to believe that the attraction, if that's what it was, growing inside his body was totally one-sided.

Although last night attraction definitely had been there—the way she'd responded to the kiss...

That was *physical* attraction, probably heightened by the danger they'd shared...

As for his country, she'd seen the inside of the palace—or a small part of it—and a ruined village, so how could she fall in love with it?

And hadn't he decided, back when he'd still had some working synapses in his brain, that what he needed in the way of a real wife was someone from his own country and background and culture?

'You haven't seen the city so I will fly you over it, but I thought for dinner we would go somewhere special. You have seen flamingos?'

'Flamingos?' she echoed in such delight he had to smile, and the tension that had captured his body began to ease. 'Big birds, long legs, pink?'

'That's them,' he told her.

'You have flamingos here? In a desert country? The leopards haven't eaten them?'

Now he laughed at her disbelief and the little joke, and his laughter dispelled the last of his tension.

'The leopards live in the mountains, the flamingos by the lagoons that are not far inland from the sea. Their habitat, too, is protected.'

He lifted off, and headed for the lights of the city, flying low above it so she could see the mix of old and new that made the capital of Al Janeen unique.

Alex peered down, fascinated by the square and rectangular buildings beneath her, the lights on the roofs showing people preparing to sleep beneath the stars, then, beyond the older area, clustered like jewels in a crown, a clutter of high-rise buildings, brilliantly lit, the new part of the city.

She turned to see this glittery grouping from another angle, then realised they were flying over nothingness again, although now she looked ahead she could see what looked like a huge, shining mirror.

'It is called Shahlah because the birds, when they are there in numbers, turn it pink, and *shahlah* means a blush.'

'A blushing lagoon? None of our fairy stories can compare with that,' Alex told him, as he set the little aircraft down far enough away from the lagoon to not disturb the birds she could now see clustered on its shore.

Were they sightseeing here?

Or had this magic land more surprises to offer her? A fancy restaurant hidden behind the dunes? She'd slipped the fine-spun cloak that went with the gown into the handbag that matched her silver sandals, just in case she needed it, but now she peered around her, she wondered if she should have brought her sneakers instead. Just how practical would silver sandals be, for walking in the sand?

Well, she could always slip them off...

Azzam opened the door and, looking at him as he stood just slightly beneath her, she felt her heart turn over. He was a good-looking man at the best of times, but out here, with the darkening dunes behind him, he *looked* like a prince—the prince of all he surveyed! Was that phrase from a fairy story as well?

He held her hand to help her from the little aircraft, easing her down, not onto the sand she had expected but—she should have guessed—onto a carpet. This one wasn't red but it was patterned and long, like a beautiful path leading her into the night. It was only as they drew near that she saw a darkened area ahead, then lights came on, revealing a long, low tent, as dark as the night itself but lit by filigree lamps, their fractured light, patterns of gold and emerald and crimson, beckoning the visitors closer.

Outside the tent, beneath one raised side of it, more carpets had been spread, with huge soft pillows like the ones in the colonnade plumped down on them.

'Madame!' Azzam said, leading her to the pillows, offering her the choice of where to sit with a sweep of his white-clad arm.

Alex sank down into the largest part of the pile, and realised they were stacked in such a way she could sit, or recline just a little. She chose to sit, bemused by the surroundings—an Ali Baba tent, flamingos turning a lake blush-pink—but not wanting to miss anything.

Which was just as well, for now soft light lit up the lagoon so she could see the pink shapes of the sleeping flamingos clearly now.

'This is a night light for viewing them in the evening, but you must come in daylight to see them picking their way through the shallow water to fully appreciate their beauty and see the mud mounds they build to lay their eggs on.'

Now Azzam had mentioned them, Alex could see the strange-looking mounds clustered together at one end of the lagoon, but although she wanted to learn more about the habits of these beautiful birds, Azzam was explaining something else— explaining the delicacies a silent servant had set down before them on a huge silver platter.

'What you might call appetisers,' he said, 'so don't eat too much or you won't want your dinner.'

Alex felt herself relaxing, although she'd been extremely nervous about this outing with Azzam, about being alone with the man who was occupying so much of her thoughts *and* disturbing her body.

'Try a date—not an ordinary date like you might buy in your supermarket but a date from the family grove. Most of our traditional food traces back to our Bedouin ancestry, when our people roamed the deserts so food had to be easily transportable.'

He was sorting through a bowl of shiny, red-brown dates as he spoke and finally selected one.

'The seed has been removed, so you can bite into it.'

He held it to her lips, and their eyes met, messages that could never be put into words passing between them—provocative messages that sent heat coursing through Alex's body.

She bit into the date, her lips just grazing the fingers that held it, so, before he took the remainder of it to his own lips, his little finger flicked her lip, making the heat spiral downwards.

You're sharing a piece of fruit, for heaven's sake, her head was yelling at her, but her body was way beyond the control of her head, whatever common sense it might be preaching at her.

A small ball of cheese came next, milky and tart, a perfect contrast to the date.

'*Labneh*,' Azzam explained. 'A cheese made from fermented goat's milk.'

He was telling her the tastes of his country, yet the words came into Alex's ears not as words of love but definitely words of seduction.

Or was she imagining it?

She had just decided she must be when he wiped the water dripping from the *labneh* off her chin then once again brushed her lips, this time with his thumb.

Her body was zinging now, so alert she felt he must be able to hear it, the way you could hear the wind through electricity wires in a storm.

And *was* she in a storm!

She should draw back, choose food for herself—the little meatball kind of things looked tasty, but now Azzam's eyes were meeting hers again and she was pinned within this sensual bubble he had woven around them, powerless to resist.

* * *

Could she feel it? Was she as aware of him as he was of her? Azzam knew he should stop feeding her, for it was also feeding his need, his hunger for this woman. Nothing could come of it, for all she was his wife. She was a visitor, heading home to her own life as soon as the children were settled.

Heading home considerably richer, he'd make sure of that, for she'd served his country well, and even *misyar* marriages demanded a dowry, although he hadn't mentioned that to her.

Because thoughts of money made him doubt her?

Not anymore!

Whatever suspicions he'd harboured about her when he'd heard of her arrival in his country had been dismissed when he'd seen her in action. He'd come to know she was giving and unselfish, not grasping and avaricious. His doubts had been destroyed by her behaviour...

He offered her the plate of *sfiha*, tiny pies, being careful not to touch her in any way now, for the conjunction of his thoughts—of wanting her and payment—had shamed him so much the fires inside him had...not died, but certainly ebbed.

He began to explain the food, pointing out how each piece was made.

'The dates, grains and legumes, along with dried fruit and nuts, were carried by the tribes, who also had their animals for milk and meat. Because the Bedu acted as guards for the caravans from India and China, they could barter for spices, although saffron was a local spice, and salt a local commodity.'

Had she stiffened when he'd touched her lips?

Alex felt the shift in the atmosphere between them, and felt a sense of loss out of all proportion to the situation, but she hid it behind questions and became fascinated by the answers as he talked of the history of his people.

They ate mysterious meat dishes, drank juices of fruits she didn't know, and finished with a type of sweet, made from yoghurt and honey, so delicious she didn't deny herself a second helping. Then the shadowy serving people were gone, vanishing as mysteriously as they had appeared, leaving another silver platter behind them, this one laden with the finest fruit. She and Azzam were alone on the carpet with moonlight touching the dunes and turning the lagoon to a shimmering silver, weaving a spell of enchantment about them.

Azzam broke the silence.

'Do you know how beautiful you are? As silver as the lagoon, as beautiful as the moon.'

He half reclined on the cushions beside her, and held a bunch of grapes above her, close to her lips.

'There is an illustration in one of our fairytales of a man feeding a woman grapes in this manner.'

Alex, bemused by the compliment he'd paid her, and still caught in the moonlight's spell, bit a grape off the bottom of the bunch and felt it explode with juice and sweetness in her mouth.

'Looking at the picture,' he said, holding the bunch above his own lips and taking one, pausing while he swallowed it, 'one imagines they are lovers.'

It's the spell, the situation, the magic of it all, Alex told herself, but her body rebelled and, aware in some instinctive way that the first move would have to come from her, she took another grape in her lips, then leant over the man beside her, transferring it to his mouth.

'Ahh...'

The soft sigh seemed to go on forever, floating above them like steam from a boiling cauldron, then Azzam's arms drew her against his body, and his lips, still tasting of grape, brushed against hers.

'I wondered if you felt it,' he whispered between kisses so light they were like the touch of the moonlight. 'For me, the attraction was so strong I thought surely you must, but you hide your feelings well, Alexandra Conroy.'

She knew no words for this situation, so she answered with a kiss, a proper kiss, capturing the lips that had been teasing hers, pressing hers against them, hard and demanding, greedy now for more, although she wasn't entirely certain what more was.

More was a response like nothing she'd ever felt or imagined, for Azzam took control of the kisses, deepening the contact by sliding his tongue along her lips, delving into her mouth, darting flickers at first, then thrusting in mimicry of what she knew was sex, although she was discovering that knowing something, even viewing it on screen, was very different to the actual thing.

His hands slid along her arms, touching her so lightly the nerve-endings shivered beneath her skin, then his hands moved to her back and explored the contours—her shoulders, sliding to her waist, finishing up on her buttocks, cupping them and pressing her against him so she felt the hardness of his erection.

Should she tell him?

Would it matter?

But how to explain the weird vows she and David had taken, as high-school kids on a youth camp, deciding marriage lay in their future so they would wait...?

David hadn't waited...

She hadn't known it at the time, hadn't even considered he might not be faithful to her, not that it worried her because once he had decamped she'd been so busy there'd been little time to think of him or his betrayal.

Now, here in the present, in the moonlight, one of Azzam's hands still held her close, while the other was moving higher, lifting her hair so he could press kisses on her neck, shifting the strap of the dress so he could kiss the skin on her shoulder.

So far, apart from that first kiss, she'd been the receiver of sensation, but now she wanted to join him in exploration. But could one remove a headdress from a prince to feel his hair? Could one slide a hand beneath the sleeve of his gown to feel his skin, and the muscles beneath it?

Sensing hesitation in the woman in his arms, Azzam drew back, turned her so she lay against the coloured cushions. With unsteady fingers, he spread the silver hair around her head.

'We are at a point, Alexandra Conroy, beyond which there will be no turning back. You must know I want nothing more than to make love to you, here in this beautiful place, in this peaceful setting. You are my wife but that does not bind you to me, neither does it mean you must consent. I would never take a woman against her wishes, but your body tells me you want this as much as I do. Am I right?'

She frowned at him, and Azzam wondered what she was thinking. Had he put it badly? Should he have asked first if she would stay here in Al Janeen and be a real wife? For he felt that things could work well between them for all his misgivings about marrying a foreigner. But telling her that might put extra pressure on her, and this woman had already done so much for his country.

Still frowning, she reached out and touched his head scarf.

'Will you take this off?' she asked, and the smile she gave him told him her answer.

'One piece of clothing each,' he challenged, and though he thought a look of shock had crossed her face, he dismissed the idea. She was a grown woman, no doubt experienced with men.

'Why not?'

She had answered his challenge but now sat up, slipping the ribbon from her hair.

He removed his headdress, then his gown, casting it down on the carpet near their feet.

'Your turn,' he said, as desire burned so fiercely inside him it was a wonder he could speak at all.

She shifted, shuffled, lifted the hem of the beautiful silver dress, then slid out lacy white undies, throwing them on top of his gown.

'That might be cheating,' he whispered, his voice husky with the hunger he felt for her. 'But I will let you get away with it and do shoe for shoe.'

He took off his sandals, setting them aside, then slid off one of hers, his hands drifting up her leg, feeling the swell of her calf, the hardness of knee bones, the soft back of her thigh.

She was shivering, her skin covered with goose-bumps, and that excited him even more, so with the removal of the second sandal he ventured further, sliding his hand high beneath the dress to touch her between her legs, feeling the soft, silken hair there, imagining it, burning to see it—

But she had stiffened, and he knew he'd gone too far, too fast. Slow down, he told himself, standing up in his *wuzar*, the white cloth his people wore as underwear, moving to be close to her again, to kiss her and touch her and feed the fires he knew burned as brightly inside her as they did within him.

She returned his kisses with a fierce need that raged through his blood, and her hands pressed against his naked back, fingers digging into his muscles, fingernails scratching against his skin, so desperate was her touch.

'The dress,' he whispered, when he knew she was riding the excitement once again.

'You do it,' she murmured back, softly acquiescent now, tremulous beneath his questing hands.

He wondered if his hands should be shaking this way as he eased the shoulder straps away, found a zip, then slowly pulled the dress down along her body so bit by bit her pearly skin, luminous in the moonlight, was revealed, and the shape of her body, of small, pert breasts, a tiny waist and swelling hips, was laid out before his gaze.

'You are beautiful.'

He breathed the words then followed them with kisses, not hard and hot but worshipful, kissing the hollow of her neck, her chest, her stomach, leaving the breasts for last then running his tongue across first one and then the other.

She moved now, abruptly at first, as if the caress had startled her, but then she lay back and reached out to pull him closer, kissing his chest as he'd kissed hers, while his hands now found a peaking nipple, and his fingers played with it, her little whimpers of delight exciting him beyond endurance.

Lost in wonder at the delight of Azzam's touch, at the magic of his kisses, at the response of her body to his exploring fingers, Alex drank it in with the thirst of someone who'd been lost too long in the desert. Her body was responding in ways she'd never imagined it could, and a tension beyond anything she'd ever felt was building up inside her.

Now his mouth had taken over the teasing of her breasts, sending fiery pulses down to the place between her legs where his hand worked a subtle new magic. He was touching her so lightly, so gently, yet the heat that had been building inside her had seemed to plateau, and she hung, suspended, in some other world.

Now his fingers probed, but gently, and she knew she must feel hot and wet for all sensation in her body was now concentrated in that one small area. His thumb moved, touched a part of her she would never have considered sensitive, yet her body jolted beneath him, like someone who'd been hit with an electric charge.

Now he calmed and soothed her again in some way—with kisses on her lips—while she wanted to scream at him to keep going, to show her exactly what she'd been missing out on all these years.

'Soon,' he whispered, as if he sensed her impatience. 'Lovemaking is too special to hurry.'

And once again he took her to that other place, but this time, as she hung there, her body taut with wanting, though what she wasn't sure, his fingers continued touching her, moving into her, his thumb again brushing her clitoris, then one more touch and the world went black, stars exploded in this inky darkness, and her body dissolved into a puddle of sensation too unbelievable for there to be words to describe it.

'Ah,' he said, nothing more, but his hand remained cupped around her and, as more tremors rent her apart, he held her safe.

But this wasn't all—she knew that—and now she'd experienced one part of this sex business she wanted all of it. Boldly she felt for him, found the iron-hard penis that had taunted her earlier, and ran exploratory fingers of her own over it. Of course she'd felt David's excitement, back when they'd been courting and sex had been a fumble in the back seat of his car, but touching David had never made her hot and anxious, never made her move restlessly against him, her body begging to be taken.

Azzam shifted until he was lying above her, his body supported on his strong arms, his undergarment gone. He was so magnificent in the moonlight she could barely breathe for the wonder of it.

'Guide me in,' he ordered, and she hurried to obey, gasping at first as her body opened to accommodate him, gasping again as a fierce thrust caused a jolt of pain, then she found the rhythm of his movements and moved with him, aware of something primal, something elemental, in this mating dance beneath the stars and moon.

But thoughts became entangled and disappeared altogether as she realised that once again she'd reached that strange plateau, but this time she knew the wonder of the experience that lay beyond it, and she moved beneath him, searching for the connection that would repeat it, moving faster, with him, rising higher, wanting the nearly unbearable tension to break again, to shatter her so she could be new again.

It came, and with it a shout of exultation from Azzam, then his movements slowed and he collapsed on top of her, his body hard and hot, slick with sweat, his lips by her ear, murmuring words she didn't understand.

She held him tightly, aware this might be the only time they could lie this way, and knew she loved him—probably would always love him. She looked up at the moon, silently telling it of her love, and knew, too, that the magic of this memory would light her life just as the moon had added magic to their lovemaking.

Azzam rolled away from her, remaining close, raising his upper body on his elbow, his head on his hand, looking down at her, his free hand running across her skin.

'You are a ghost, an apparition, a thing of wonder and delight. That is what I said to you in my language.'

Now he touched her face.

'You are happy? No regrets?'

Still lost in a place beyond words, she smiled and shook her head, then, as if remembering something, he frowned.

'Alex?'

Her name was more tentative on his lips than she had ever heard it, then, still frowning he ran his hand down her body, sliding it between her legs, touching the wetness lingering there.

Now he frowned, as if remembering something, studying her, the frown deepening.

'You were a virgin?'

It was more an accusation than a question and it cut into her hazy, drifting thoughts, bringing her back to earth with such a jolt she sat up and stared at him.

'Is that a sin?' she demanded, so annoyed at being shaken out of her little bubble of happiness she could have slapped him.

'Not a sin, no,' he said quietly, touching her on the shoulder. 'But you should have said— I could have hurt you— I wouldn't—'

'If you say you wouldn't have had sex with me if you'd known, I *might* just hit you,' she warned. 'And if you mention it again—as if I had some kind of rare sexually transmitted disease—I will walk home from this place if it takes me all night.'

Angry and feeling somehow humiliated, as if her virginity had been an affront to him, she reached out and grabbed the first thing that came to hand, which happened to be his gown. Clutching it in front of her, she moved away from him.

'Alex!'

Azzam said her name but had no words with which to follow it. Somehow, on top of what had happened, he'd made it worse—offended her in some way he didn't understand.

'Well?' she demanded, his gown wrapped around her body, tucked in above her breasts so she wore it like a sarong while she searched among the tumbled cushions, presumably for her gown and underwear.

'I don't know what to say,' he admitted. 'I don't know what to tell you. I want to say I'm sorry, but I'm not, for what we shared was, to me, truly amazing—something very special and something I will always remember.'

'Then that makes two of us,' she snapped, finding her gown. Discarding his robe, she pulled the silver sheath over her head. But she wasn't done. Grabbing the small silver bag she'd brought with her, she pulled out a cloak. In the haze of what was happening, Azzam still registered the fact that it must have been silk for it to have folded so small. Now she'd donned it over the silver dress and stood, a slender, muted figure all in black, the milky white skin no longer tantalising him, although the shining hair still shamed the moon with its beauty.

'You are still you beneath the gown and cloak,' he reminded her, but she didn't speak and he knew he'd broken the bond between them—a bond he'd been beginning to believe might form a solid foundation for something special.

CHAPTER NINE

THEY flew back to the palace in silence, Azzam wondering if he'd ever understand women. From the helipad behind the palace he could walk her as far as the door to the women's house where she was staying, or to his own quarters—equidistant.

He wanted to do the latter, not because he had any intention of making love to her again this evening but so they could talk and maybe sort this out. But how to ask? The woman was a puzzle to him, an enigma! She must be, what, late twenties? And undoubtedly there were plenty of women of her age who were still virgins, but a woman as beautiful and desirable as she was?

He shook his head, further thought beyond him.

'I don't like to part like this,' he said, when they were on the ground, the engine off and the blades slowing. 'Would you come with me to somewhere we can talk—only talk? I realise you are upset, and with me, but whatever I said it was inadvertent. The experience we shared was very special to me, more special than I can put into words.'

The black-garbed figure shrugged her shoulders.

'I don't think there's anything to talk about,' she finally said. 'After all, I'll be gone before long. As soon as the children are settled I'll be leaving.'

The cool, offhand statement thudded into Azzam's belly like a punch from an assailant and desperation grew within him.

'We could talk about that—about your plans,' he said. 'Must you go so soon? Might you not stay a while, see my country, learn a little of its ways—maybe stay—'

He'd been about to say 'forever' but had pulled back the word at the last moment, thinking it might frighten her. Women needed to be wooed, not hit with marriage proposals out of the blue. And though they were technically married, he was beginning to realise that what he wanted with this woman was a real marriage…

What had he been about to say? Maybe

stay—what? Alex found herself pondering this to stop herself thinking of other things. Like the pathetic way she'd reacted to the virgin thing out there in the desert! Like the way her body was behaving as if the coldness between them didn't exist. Beyond all reason, it was yearning for his touch, and the excitement of his lovemaking...

'I don't think talking will help,' she finally replied, knowing the more she was in this man's presence the less likely she'd be to get over this yearning business. Discovering she was in love with him had been one thing, but discovering what his body could do to hers, that was entirely different. She could hide her love, but was she strong enough to control these new urges of her body, and if she gave in to them, wouldn't he guess the other part?

'Perhaps tomorrow,' he said, his voice sounding strange—hoarse? Strained?

'Perhaps,' she agreed, lying through her teeth, knowing she would do everything in her power to avoid him and, if it was impossible, to see him only in the company of others.

He climbed out of the helicopter and walked

around to help her out. She held the cloak around her as if it was armour that might somehow protect her, but he put his hands on her waist and lifted her easily from her seat, and the heat of his hands burned through the layers of cloth so she felt as if he'd branded her, the outline of his fingers burned into her skin.

He walked with her to the rear door she now knew led to her quarters, and spoke quietly to a man who sat nearby. The man slid off into the shadows, and Azzam stood with her, this time resting his hands on her shoulders and peering into her face.

'You won't change your mind? Won't sit with me a while and talk?'

'No, thank you!'

She knew she sounded tetchy but she was feeling that way too, for the man's hands on her had reawakened the barely diminished fires of earlier and her body clamoured to lean into his, to feel his contours—to know him...

'Then there is only one thing left to say,' he said, with the smile she'd seen so rarely, but which had the power to light up her heart.

'And that's goodnight,' he murmured, and before she could retreat he bent his head and kissed her lips, the softness of his skin accentuating the hard demand behind that simple kiss. Her heart rate soared and imps danced in her head, distracting her from the common sense she knew she needed—desperately.

Now her body was leaning into his, the kiss was deepening, and the longing to be with him, naked, feeling all of him, was all but overwhelming her. Then one small thread of common sense came through for her. If this was how she felt after making love one time, how much worse would it be after two—or four—or fifteen…?

She broke away. What was the point? She didn't want an affair with this man. She didn't want it to be *more* difficult to leave this country. Already it would be bad enough, leaving Samarah and the children, whom she was coming to love.

He released her, and it was only in her foolish heart she felt reluctance in the release.

'We *will* talk,' he said, opening the door for her, waiting until a young woman appeared then speaking to her, no doubt asking her to see Alex to her room.

'Goodnight,' she said, though with sadness. But what else was there to say?

'Goodnight,' he echoed, then he walked away.

Alex followed the young woman to her room, then shooed her away, assuring her she could undress herself. She stripped off the cloak, then the silver dress, casting it into a heap on the floor, wanting to bundle it up and drop it into a rubbish bin then wanting to see it cleaned so she might take it home as a reminder of a magical, if thoroughly disturbing night.

Seeing herself in the mirror made her grimace, faint red marks that would turn to bruises on her limbs and body. But remembering how they'd got there, remembering the pleasure the man had generated in her body, she couldn't regret anything that had happened. The only regret she had for was the way it had ended. But how else could it have ended? There could be no affair—she was going home—and that was quite apart from the fact that for some reason he hadn't liked her being a virgin.

Well, bother him!

She went to bed, wondering if sleep would come, her body more alert, more wired than it had ever been.

Sleep came.

She woke to sunshine making patterns on the silk coverlet again, and she stretched, lazily, a little sore, but with no regrets.

Sitting up in bed, she realised she had company. Tasnim was sitting by the door, the child as silent as she usually was. Alex opened her arms and the girl ran into them, hugging her tightly, then she slipped off the bed and went away, returning with Zahid and the baby, Masun.

'All my family,' Alex joked, as she hugged them all, then waggled the baby in the air so he crowed with laughter. If only they *could* be her family—*her* laughing, happy children.

Impossible!

A selfish dream...

But one that bit in deep, probably because her own family was all but gone, leaving behind such pain and hardship...

Ghaada was by the door now, and she translated as Tasnim and Zahid rattled on, telling Alex the car was waiting, they were going in a car, please could she come.

Now!

Alex laughed. Typical family! The children had been waiting, not to see her but to go for a ride in a car, obviously something new for them. Ghaada took them out of the room so Alex could dress, reminding the children Alex also had to have her breakfast.

'I will keep the baby here,' she said to Alex, 'for the car would be too tiring for him and you do not need the distraction.'

'But I thought you could accompany us and tell me what I am seeing,' Alex said, and Ghaada shook her head.

'As well as a driver, His Highness has arranged a—is it tour guide you say? He has planned the tour for you and told this young woman where she is to take you. Hafa will bring your breakfast, and the car is waiting when you are ready.'

Soon after Ghaada and the children departed,

Hafa entered, carrying a tray with a coffee pot, a cup, sugar and sweet pastries on it.

'I select an outfit for you?' she asked, as Alex sat down to breakfast, surprised at how hungry she was feeling.

'I think for sightseeing my own jeans and shirt,' Alex told her, determined to get her mind off the children and dreams of a new family, and into 'going home' mode.

Hafa seemed about to argue, but in the end she disappeared into the dressing room, returning with the clothes Alex had been wearing when she'd left Australia what seemed like a lifetime ago.

Their tour guide spoke perfect English, acquired, she explained, because she'd grown up in England where her father had run the European end of one of the royal family's businesses. They went first to the markets in the old part of town, where Alex was dazzled by the multitude of aromas—herbs, spices, strange fruit and the ever-present frankincense. But a riot of colour also assaulted her senses, for the vivid yellow of open bags of turmeric powder and the deeper gold of saffron, the bright sheens of bolts of colourful silk, draped across stalls piled high with goods.

The children oohed and aahed as any children would, seeing such an array of goods spread out on either side of narrow alleys. They reached the area where metal objects—pots and pans, urns, vases and lamps—were sold, and Alex stopped to look more carefully. Surely she was entitled to take home one small memento, and if she could discover a small, shapely lamp like the one Tasnim had found, it would be the ideal souvenir.

And she could dream of wishes…

The children poked around among the treasures and it was Zahid who found a tiny lamp, holding it up to show Tasnim, no doubt commenting on how like hers it was. He held it out to Alex, who turned to the guide.

'Can you ask how much—?'

She stopped, an unbelievable awareness striking her. She had no money! Not even Australian money, for her wallet was back at the palace, the last thing she'd thought she'd need.

'It is very cheap,' their guide told her, mentioning a sum in Al Janeen money that meant nothing to Alex.

'No, it doesn't matter,' Alex told her, and she hustled the children on to the next stall, and the next, through the markets and back to the car, her mind in a whirl as she came to terms with just how isolated she was and how totally dependent on Azzam's goodwill to get back home.

Although Samarah would surely help if Azzam's promise to arrange her flight home didn't eventuate—

No way! The thought of borrowing from her kind friend was too much. Bad enough she'd had to ask Azzam for wages.

They drove through the city, visited a museum that had reminders of the past, beautifully bejewelled camel saddles, magnificent gowns and exotic headdresses. Pictures of a distant past were arrayed along the walls, showing nomad camps, and herds of goats summering in the mountains— maybe not far from the children's village. Also on the walls, photographic portraits of memorable faces, ordinary people going about their lives but with the strong, proud profiles of their race, the same profile Alex so admired in Azzam.

Eventually, when the children tired, Alex suggested they return home.

'One more stop,' their tour guide said, and now the big black limo left the city streets, heading out on a bitumen road across the desert. They drove for maybe an hour, then crested a dune and there beneath them spread the shining lagoon, pink around the edges with the daintily stepping flamingos.

'The blushing lake,' the guide said, as the children gazed in wonder at the birds. Alex was less interested in them, orienting herself by the nest mounds but seeing no sign of the tent in which she'd spent such a memorable evening. Wasn't there a saying about desert people folding their tents and disappearing into the night?

Yet her memories couldn't be folded away so easily, and a physical ache started up inside her as she longed to be back at the beginning of the magical night and maybe handling it all differently.

Better—oh, certainly better—for didn't everyone make things better in their dreams?

Both children fell asleep as they drove back to the palace, and Ghaada appeared when the vehicle pulled up, so she carried Zahid while Alex, after thanking their guide, carried Tasnim, feeling the girl's slight body against her breast, feeling the love that had crept into her heart where these children were concerned.

It was a different love from the other love in there—the one that had slammed in without warning over what was a matter of days.

Could love happen like that?

So quickly?

Maybe it wasn't love. Maybe it was nothing more than a strong physical attraction.

But as Alex left the sleeping Tasnim on her bed and returned to her own quarters, she knew that was wrong. Yes, she was physically attracted to the man—even more so after last night—but what she felt was more than that. It was a mix of admiration and respect and something that she couldn't explain—some inner connection to the man—as if they were linked in the way speakers on phones in distant places were linked—brought together by some unseen, and to most people mysterious, power.

Hafa was waiting for her, with a message that Samarah would see her and the children in the colonnade at the usual time.

Alex thanked her and sent her away, assuring the kind young woman she could bath and dress herself, wanting to be alone for a while with her straying thoughts. But being alone didn't help make sense of the chaos in her head, neither did it soothe the agitation of her body, although maybe Azzam wouldn't be in the group at the colonnade this evening.

She lay on her bed, studying the marble fretwork of the window, marvelling as always at the talent of the master craftsman who must have carved it, thinking about shifting patterns to distract her mind and body. The knock on the door was louder than Ghaada's or Hafa's usual light tap, but without stirring much Alex called, 'Come in.'

To her surprise it was Clarice who swept into her room, cast a knowing eye around it, and sniffed in a way that suggested the sumptuous suite was only a small step up from servant's quarters.

'I thought as we're both strangers in this land—although I've been here long enough to be accepted and adored by the locals—we should get to know each other.'

Alex sat up on the edge of the bed, but before she could offer Clarice a chair, the woman had sat down by the window, where the play of light made patterns on her skin, illuminating her golden beauty.

'I'm going home any day now,' Alex told her, then realised it might have sounded rude, so she quickly added, 'not that I wouldn't want to be friends with you, but as I say...'

She left the sentence hanging.

'Really?' Clarice said, and it seemed to Alex that there was relief in the word, although it was a mystery why Alex's departure should please Clarice.

'Once the children are settled here,' Alex expanded, 'I'll be free to go. It just seemed wrong to take them from their village and dump them

244 SHEIKH, CHILDREN'S DOCTOR...HUSBAND

somewhere strange without a little bit of time for them to adjust.'

Clarice looked perplexed, or as perplexed as someone who had very little in the way of facial expressions could look. Her eyebrows had moved as if to come together in a frown, but no lines marred her smooth forehead.

'But why would you care?' she asked. 'You didn't know the children and they barely know you and they must be so delighted to get out of their squalid little village and come to live in a palace, they wouldn't care who looked after them.'

The local people adored someone who spoke of 'squalid little villages'?

Alex pushed the thought away and concentrated on the main issue.

'These children have lost their mother. No matter where they came from or how magnificent their current circumstances might be, they are grieving and need time to adjust to the worst loss a child can suffer. They need to feel secure in their surroundings, and to know they can trust the adults around them. They need to feel wanted and

loved and to know that their little family won't
be split up.'

Clarice stretched and ran a hand through her
glorious mane of hair.

'Sounds like a load of psychological claptrap
to me,' she said. 'Kids are kids, they adapt.'

Swallowing the growl that rose in her throat,
Alex rose from the bed.

'I really need to shower. Was there something
else you wanted?'

Clarice seemed put out.

'I only came to chat,' she said. 'With Bahir
gone, there's no one in this place I can talk to.
I should just get out of here—go home to the
States, I've houses there—but there's this mourning thing they do and I don't want to upset everyone in case I want to come back some day.'

Alex sat down again. The words sounded
false, somehow, but the woman *was* recently
bereaved.

'I am sorry for your loss.' It was a trite statement, but Alex meant it.

Clarice waved it away.

'I gather you made a *misyar* marriage with

Azzam while you were out there at the earth-quake place,' she said, and Alex wondered if that was what her visitor had come to discuss.

'Apparently it was the only thing to do,' she answered, hoping she sounded calmer than she felt because whatever had happened between Azzam and herself was not only private but also precious in a way she didn't fully understand.

'Oh, yes,' her visitor agreed, rather too readily. 'He couldn't have had his reputation tarnished by sharing a tent with a foreigner. Of course, no marriage in these parts, even a *misyar* marriage, is legal until it's consummated.'

Alex's breathing stopped, and her heart stood still, then picked up and raced, while small, shallow breaths saved her from passing out completely.

Had Clarice seen her reaction?

Alex sincerely hoped not, but the statement had raised so many questions in Alex's head that she needed to get rid of the woman so she could at least *try* to sort through them.

Realising some kind of reply was needed, she shrugged her shoulders.

'I wouldn't know about any of that,' she said, hoping she sounded a lot more casual than she felt. 'Now, I really must shower and dress. Samarah wants to see the children.'

Now Clarice stood up.

'Oh, well, whatever Samarah wants Samarah must have,' she said, not even attempting to hide the bitchiness in the words. And on that note she swept out of the room.

Alex lay back on the bed.

Azzam would have known this thing about marriage and consummation.

She'd sensed the previous afternoon in the colonnade that he was using her against Clarice in some way.

Introducing her as his wife.

When, apparently, she wasn't his wife.

Was that why he'd taken her to that magical place last night?

Was that why he'd seduced her?

Be honest, she told herself, it had hardly been a seduction—she'd wanted it as much as he had.

Maybe more?

She sighed and rolled over on her stomach,

pressing her hot face into the pillows, aware of how little she knew of male-female relationships, aware of how lost she was...

She'd go home. The children would adapt. They were already at ease with Ghaada, for Alex had seen them laughing and playing with her in the courtyard gardens, and Samarah would give them love. They would be all right.

She heaved herself off the bed, showered hurriedly, then stood in front of the wardrobe. Much as she'd have loved to put on her jeans and a clean shirt, she didn't want to hurt Samarah's feelings by not wearing one of her gifts.

Sorting through them, she found a pale pink tunic and trousers, less fancy than the other sets, although once she was dressed she realised the pink material took on a life of its own, deepening in colour in the folds, paling almost to white where it crossed her breasts and hips.

It was beautiful and a tiny little bit of her was glad because *she* looked beautiful in it—or as beautiful as someone as nondescript as she was ever could look. She hooked her hair up using two of the jewelled combs from the bathroom, wrapped a scarf around her head and once again put pale pink lipstick on her lips.

The children came bounding in just as she finished and she knew from their excited chatter that they were complimenting her. Ghaada translated their exuberant comments so Alex was blushing as she made her way with them, Ghaada carrying Masun today, along the colonnade to where Samarah held her daily court.

In Alex's mind, as she approached the gathering, she had it sorted that she didn't want Azzam to be there, but when she saw him, seated beside his mother, her heart gave a treacherous little leap, and warmth flooded recently excited parts of her body. Breathing deeply so she appeared calm and focussed, she greeted Samarah, nodded hello to Azzam as if he hadn't ignited her body in ways she still couldn't believe possible the night before, then urged the children forward to greet both adults.

Zahid greeted Azzam like an old friend and showed him a treasure he had found—a small white stone from the lagoon—while Tasnim drew close to Samarah, who lifted the child onto her lap and gave her a hug.

'I am blessed to have these children in my life,' Samarah said. 'Last night I read to them before they went to sleep. I had forgotten what a simple joy that was.'

Hearing Samarah's sincerity in the simple words, Alex could only smile, certain that the children had found a secure home here at the palace and a very special guardian in Samarah.

'I, too, have something special,' Azzam said, and, thinking he was speaking to Zahid, Alex barely glanced his way, but he was handing a little lamp to Zahid, speaking to him in his own language, although when the little boy came and shyly presented the lamp to her, Alex could only stare—first at it, and then at Azzam.

'The guide told me you admired one,' he said, as she turned it around in her hands, looking at it from all angles, aware that it was very different from the market lamp, yet not understanding how.

'It's beautiful,' she said, 'but it looks expensive. I can't accept expensive gifts from you.'

Samarah waved away her protest.

'You are his wife so he can give you anything—far better things than an old lamp—although I suspect objects, possessions aren't as important to you as people, isn't that so?'

'Not important at all,' Alex assured her, remembering how it had been the need for possessions—a fine house for his wife, good art works, the best furniture—that had started Rob's gambling.

Azzam had watched her approach, drinking in the sight of her. She'd tied a pale pink scarf across her head, the material so fine he could see, beneath it, the combs she'd used to hold her hair back from her face.

She'd looked so serenely beautiful his mouth had gone dry and he'd wondered if he'd be able to speak to her at all, let alone say the things he wanted to say.

Now he watched her turning the lamp in her hands, answering his mother, rejecting any wish to have possessions. Something in her past has made her this way—not only about possessions, but had made her remote, untrusting, Azzam decided.

If he managed to speak, how could he bridge the gap between them—a gap he very definitely wanted to bridge?

He accepted that they barely knew each other, but he believed the bond between them, forged in the chaos of the disaster, was rare and special, something that should be nurtured so it could grow and flourish into a deeply loving marriage.

But he'd upset her, and she'd drawn away, and he had no idea how to bring her close again. He watched her, still studying the little lamp—a trinket, nothing more—and wondered what she'd think if he told her he'd, foolishly he knew, already wished on it—wished for her to stay here in Al Janeen, to stay as his wife and consort.

Ask her, his mother had said when he'd sought her advice, but how to ask? When?

She held the lamp, showing it to the children, then smiled at him, a smile that seemed to rip his heart apart, so much did it hurt him.

'Thank you. It will be a wonderful reminder of Al Janeen for me to take home with me.'

'Must you go?'

Really smooth move, brother, the ghost of

Bahir teased, but desperation had prompted the words.

Now she smiled again, a sad smile this time that tore a bit more of his heart.

'You know I must. Originally I came to tend Samarah on the flight—I've already stayed longer than I should.'

'There is family back at home? You miss them? Is that why you are so determined to leave us?'

He was saying this all wrong, but he badly needed to know she had pressing reasons to go— apart, of course, from putting a vast distance between herself and him.

'Family obligations,' she replied, not meeting his eyes but with enough emotion in her face for him to know it hurt her to say it. Because she didn't want to leave?

Or maybe it was the obligation that hurt her?

How could that be?

He wanted to know more.

Put bluntly, he wanted to know everything about her, but for him to learn about her, and she about him, she had to stay.

254 SHEIKH, CHILDREN'S DOCTOR...HUSBAND

Could he order it? Wasn't he the ruler—couldn't he command it?

Command this woman?

Of course he couldn't. Not her or any other woman, realistically...

'But now you have obligations here, too,' he said, speaking quietly, although his mother's women friends had withdrawn, taking the children into the garden so only he, Alex and his mother remained on the carpets. 'There are the children, and as my...'

He hesitated before saying the word 'wife', knowing it wasn't right for he'd told her there'd be no strings attached to their *misyar* marriage but desperate to get her to change her mind about leaving. Fortunately, before the word came out, Clarice had appeared, coming to stand beside him, taking his arm, urging him a little apart.

'This conversation isn't finished,' he said to Alex, then he followed Clarice a little way along the colonnade.

'Your mother is finding happiness in the children,' she began, and Azzam wondered where the conversation was leading for Clarice rarely gave a thought to other people's happiness.

'She is,' he replied. 'I think it takes her mind off her loss.'

Clarice smiled at him—more a smirk than a smile for it sent coolness through his blood.

'Then perhaps soon I will give her more pleasure—the greatest pleasure of all. I'll give her a child with real meaning for her.'

He heard the words but they made little sense, but as he turned to look at her he saw she was patting her stomach and looking unbearably pleased with herself.

'You're pregnant?'

He spoke quietly, not wanting to raise false hope in his mother, should she hear the quiet conversation.

'It would seem so,' Clarice said, but now the smile he'd once let light his world seemed smug and even devious.

'That would be good news indeed,' he said, wondering why he was feeling so doubtful.

'The child, if it's a boy, will be the true heir, of course.'

She was looking at him now, as if the words might hold some hidden meaning.

Did she think it would hurt him? That he might resent his brother's child? How could he, he who'd loved Bahir better than himself?

Of course Bahir's son would be the heir. Perhaps, even, should the child be a girl, his country would have grown enough to accept *her* as the ruler. Such a time, he was sure, wasn't that far away.

But Clarice was still talking to him, standing a little behind him and speaking quietly so no one else would hear the conversation.

'That's the real reason I thought we should marry, you and I. That way the succession is protected. Bahir's child grows up as yours, and becomes the prince in due time.'

The conversation that had begun, he felt, at the worst possible time, had now taken such a truly outlandish turn that it took him a moment to get his head around it.

'We do not have to be married for the child to grow up to be the ruler,' he told her. 'Bahir's child would be the heir, my place that of a regent until he was of age.'

'And if I were to marry someone else? Take my child back to my homeland of America so he grows up there? How would that suit your ideas of national identity?'

Cold fear gripped him as he realised what the woman was doing. She was bartering with the life of her unborn child, for how could a child raised in another country understand the people and the land he was born to rule?

And how could he allow Bahir's child to be raised by another man—particularly the kind of man Clarice, now she had more than enough money than she would need to keep her in style for life, might choose?

He took her arm and led her down into the garden courtyard, staying away from the children and in the shade of trees for the sun was still hot. But for all the heat, his body shivered as the dreams he'd spun of a real marriage between himself and Alex vanished into the ether, dreams of love crumbling to dust beneath his feet, lost forever because of the obligation of family.

The obligation he felt towards his beloved brother, his twin, his other half…

CHAPTER TEN

THIS conversation isn't finished. Wasn't that what he'd said? Yet he'd walked away with Clarice. Alex excused herself to Samarah and went to play with the children in the garden, chasing the two older ones around the beautifully crafted hedges and topiary shaped as balls. Tired at last, she sat on the edge of the fountain and took Masun from Ghaada, dabbling his feet in the water, making him laugh, his innocent chuckles bruising her heart because she would never see him grow up.

'It is time for the children's dinner,' Ghaada said, taking the now sleepy baby from Alex and leading the children back to their rooms.

Alex remained by the fountain. Trailing her fingers in the water, drinking in the peace of the tranquil setting, seeing the fierce red sun dropping below the high walls of the palace. Darkness fell swiftly and she saw the women moving back towards the building that housed them, next to what she now knew was the visitors' building, where she and the children had rooms. Looking around, she realised it was more a series of houses than one large palace, for there were other buildings she didn't know, but all were linked by the colonnade.

One would be Azzam's, of course, and presumably Clarice still lived in what had been Bahir's building, and from what Samarah had said, there were receiving areas where people came to meet their prince, and places where dignitaries were entertained. There were areas also for servants and old family retainers, and for cousins and aunts and the women who were friends. Alex was considering how reassuring it must be, this self-enclosed community, how safe people must feel within it, when she felt, rather than saw, Azzam approach.

'I thought you would be eating with my mother,' he said quietly, sitting beside her but not touching her. Not that touch was needed, for awareness was flaring between them with a galvanic power that singed the skin and burned along the nerves.

On her side, anyway...

'I wanted to see the sun set,' Alex told him, unwilling to admit she'd been lost in thoughts of safeness and community.

'And I need to talk to you, but I find I have no words for what I want to say, or, now, the right to say them,' he said quietly. He took one of her hands in both of his, and held it, warm and—yes, safe!

'I would have asked you to stay,' he said then he gave a short, abrupt laugh. 'Asked? How stupid! I probably would have begged you to stay.'

He turned her hand over and dropped a kiss into the palm, then folded her fingers over it to keep the kiss, the hand again held between his.

'But circumstances have changed and I cannot tell you things I would have said. For that, I am truly sorry. But know that when you go, and it can be tomorrow if you wish, you will take a piece of me with you.'

A feeling akin to panic flashed along Alex's nerves and she stood up, moving slightly away, then turning back towards him because she was puzzled as well, and aching with her love for him.

'Is this to do with my overreaction last night? Is it because of that you cannot talk?'

He stood up, put his hands lightly on her shoulders, and looked down into her face.

'It is not to do with you, but with a—a constraint I suppose you would call it, put on me by family obligations.'

For a moment Alex thought he might kiss her, then he muttered what sounded like an oath of some kind and walked away, heading for a shadowy part of the garden she hadn't yet explored.

Drawn by the pain she'd heard in the words, she followed, finding him beside an ancient, black-trunked, gnarled old tree.

'This tree was here before the palace—here before my ancestors first camped in this place. It symbolises continuation, shows us that life goes on no matter what. It is frankincense—you know it?'

Alex came forward and touched the rough trunk.

'I know the scent of it now,' she said. 'It's everywhere.'

'It made our fortune in the early days—not just this tree but many like it. They grow in only a few places. Here, feel the trunk.'

He took her hand and held it against the rough bark, pressing her fingers into what seemed like a cut in it.

'The frankincense gatherers cut through the rough bark to the living tree beneath and it bleeds. Can you feel the small lump there? We call it a tear, as if the tree cries with pain yet its pain gives us life in the same way as a mother's pain gives life to her child.'

He took his hand away and Alex looked up at the night sky through the fine silvery leaves of the ancient tree, wondering exactly what Azzam had been telling her, knowing it was important to him.

Now, as she watched, he pulled a small pen-knife from his pocket and again ran his hands across the bark of the tree, feeling for a cut perhaps, because when he turned back to her he had two small, clear, tear-shaped lumps of frankincense which he pressed into her hands.

'You take my tears with you when you go,' he said quietly, 'and also my heart.'

Alex closed her fingers tightly around the little buds, and was trying to make sense of his words when he bent and kissed her lightly on the lips, before disappearing as quietly as he had come.

Alex stayed beneath the tree, the tears of frankincense biting into her palm, until the sky was dark enough to see the stars. She tried to find the constellations Azzam had pointed out to her, but their brightness was blurred by the tears that had filled her eyes.

Eventually she made her way back to her room, where Hafa scolded her for sitting outside when the cool night air was descending. Waving away the young woman's concern and fending off offers of dinner—food was the last thing her churning stomach would accept—she went into the dressing room and found the jeans and shirt she'd put on one morning that seemed an aeon ago.

'You can go home tomorrow if you wish.' Wasn't that what Azzam had said?

She didn't wish to but she had to go sometime and the way she was feeling, the sooner she made the break, not only from him but from the children and Samarah, the easier it would be.

She *would* go tomorrow…

She put out the jeans and shirt, telling herself she'd leave in her own clothes, set her socks and sneakers beside them, aware how pathetic they looked on the chair in the sumptuous dressing room. She was contemplating a shower when a knock on the bedroom door sent her back in that direction.

Clarice!

'Hi!' she said, breezing in as if they were best of friends. 'Azzam said you're leaving soon so I thought I'd say good-bye and offer a suggestion. I was going to fly home to the States to see my folks tomorrow, but things have changed so the plane is free. I know the pilot well. Shall I let him know you'll go tomorrow? The plane's all fuelled up and the staff on standby so it's a shame not to use it.'

Had Azzam sent her?

Was this what he'd wanted to say but couldn't?

Pain filled Alex's body but there was no way she was going to show it.

'If that suits Azzam and the rest of the family, tomorrow would suit me too,' she said, enunciating each word carefully in case a careless syllable might open the floodgates of her pain.

'I'll arrange it all and send someone to let you know when the car will pick you up,' Clarice told her, smiling brightly as if she'd just accomplished some difficult mission.

Hafa returned as Clarice departed, bringing a tray with juice and fruit on it.

'You must eat something,' she told Alex, and to please her Alex took a piece of melon, but she knew she'd never get it down past the wedge of sadness in her throat.

'I am leaving tomorrow,' she told Hafa, who cried out and waved her hands, chattering half in her native language and half in English, obviously not happy about it.

'I would like to see Samarah before I go. Would it be best now or in the morning, early?'

Hafa frowned then shook her head, finally going across to the phone and phoning someone, talking volubly with much hand-waving.

'Samarah's woman said to come now. They have finished dinner and are having fruit and sweets. You will join them?'

How could she not? Alex thought. Samarah had become a friend.

'I don't think I like goodbyes,' she said to Hafa as the young woman led her to Samarah's rooms. 'I'm not used to them.'

'But you will return,' Hafa said. 'You will want to see the children, and maybe the village when it is rebuilt.'

And risk seeing Azzam?

Risk renewed pain when just maybe some of the wounds she could feel now in her heart were healing over?

'I don't think so,' she said, but so quietly perhaps Hafa didn't hear her.

'There are visitors,' Hafa explained as they entered the big room. 'They came late but will take sweetmeats with us, as will you.'

Hafa led her to what Alex now realised was a

privileged position by Samarah's side. Alex sank down onto a cushion, and smiled at the older woman, who was looking so much better since she'd returned home. Except her dark eyes were concerned and worry creased her forehead.

She touched Alex's hand.

'I am sorry you are leaving,' she said quietly. 'Sorry in too many ways to tell you. My son, I think, is making a mistake, but a mother cannot do more than guide her children, she cannot bend them to her will.'

'I am sorry to hear that,' Alex said, giving Samarah's fingers a little squeeze, wondering what Azzam had done to make his mother looked so worried. 'But he is a good son, you know that,' she added, hoping to reassure the woman.

'Yes, perhaps too good,' Samarah said, then to Alex's surprise she leaned forward and pressed a kiss on Alex's cheek. 'We will meet again, my dear,' she said. 'The genie in the lamp has promised me this.'

And reaching into the folds of her tunic, she pulled out the little lamp and handed it to Alex.

'You left it in the colonnade when you played

with the children, but I kept it safe for you, as I will keep the children safe. You may be sure of that.'

Tears were brimming in Alex's eyes again, and the lump in her throat now made speech impossible. She gave Samarah's hand one last squeeze, then stood up and moved towards the door, Hafa behind her, chattering about the children, but Alex's head was too full of sadness to hear the words.

After six weeks back at work it seemed to Alex as if she'd never been away. One day slid into the next. She worked night shifts at the hospital, day shifts at the clinic, slowly but steadily reducing Rob's debt.

She hadn't heard from the money-lender so she'd assumed Azzam had been as good as his word and transferred a week's wages into her account to cover the payment that would have been taken out while she was away. One day she'd have to check the figures, so she'd know how much she had in reserve for an emergency, but right now doing anything apart from going to work, doing her job and coming home was beyond her.

She picked up the little lamp and rattled the tears of frankincense she kept inside it, the only tangible reminders of that magical time. She touched the lamp gently, wanting to rub it, to find a genie, to make a wish…

But what wish?

Not money, that was for sure. She'd pay off Rob's debts in time. No, what she'd wish for was impossible, for how could Azzam suddenly appear in her tiny bed-sit?

Yet her hands still held the lamp, feeling its warmth, wondering if wishes might come—

The sharp knock on the door made her drop the precious object, but she caught it before it hit the floor and she put it down safely on the small table before going to see who was there. Working the hours she did, she rarely socialised, and never had visitors, not ashamed of her tiny home but aware that even two people made it feel crowded.

Azzam barged through the door then stared around him in amazement, before turning to stare at her in what looked very like disbelief.

'Why are you living like this?' he demanded, anger she didn't understand written clearly on his usually inscrutable features.

Not that she was understanding much of anything. What was he doing there? How had he found her? What did he want?

Of course she hadn't rubbed the lamp!

'It's my home,' she managed, eventually, but apparently that didn't satisfy him, for he took a turn, three strides, around the small space and faced her again.

'Your home? What are you? Some kind of stoic? Are you doing penance for some unnameable sin? You have a million dollars in the bank and you live like this? Ah, it's that you won't touch my money! That's it, isn't it? Do you feel I did you such wrong you won't accept it from me? Well, let me tell you, *misyar* marriage or not, you were entitled to a dowry! It is *your* money, Alex, not a gift but an official dowry such as is required by law.'

Alex had slumped onto the end of her divan when he'd mentioned the money in the bank, and her mind had stopped working about then.

However, he was looming over her, still angry, but looking down now as if he expected some kind of answer.

There was only one thing she *could* say.

'*What* million dollars?'

Maybe two things.

'*What* bank?'

All that did was make him angrier, for this time he whirled faster in his pacing around the room while she battled the silly delight dancing in her heart at the sight of him.

'You don't know?' he growled as he came past her again. 'Do you never check your account?'

'My bank account?' Alex queried, but faintly, as it was hard to get her brain working on this subject when it was busy trying to stop her heart misbehaving. 'My pay goes into it and my expenses come out of it by automatic transfer. I usually know, maybe not to the cent, about how much I have in there. A couple of hundred dollars for emergencies—I always try to keep that.'

Azzam shook his head. He'd come to ask Alex to marry him—to be his wife forever—but first he'd had to practically force the woman at the clinic where she worked to give him Alex's address, and now he'd walked into a room smaller than his dressing room, to find it was her home. Now she was telling him she tried to keep a couple of hundred dollars in the bank for emergencies. This was poverty...

'You're a doctor, you earn good money, yet you try to keep a couple of hundred dollars in the bank for emergencies. Where does your money go, Alex? What is this obligation you spoke of that forces you to live like this?'

Wrong question and big mistake! Fire flashed in her pale eyes and she stood up, tall and proud in front of him, confronting him just as she had in the rose garden so long ago.

'That is none of your business,' she said, her small, determined chin tilted towards him, eminently kissable lips right there.

Which was when his anger died away!

'Oh, but it is,' he whispered, and he leaned forward and brushed the lightest of kisses on those irresistible lips. Then, as she'd neither slapped his face, nor moved away, he put his arms around her and tucked her slight body up against his, holding the precious woman he'd so nearly lost close to his heart.

'You see, I love you,' he said, because there didn't seem any other way to say it. 'Love you so much that to walk in here and see you living like this, I was shocked and hurt and angry. And if you want the truth, because I was so uncertain coming here, so afraid I wouldn't find you, or worse, find that you didn't love me, anger took over.'

She squirmed against him and he realised he was holding her far too tightly. He eased his grasp and she looked up at him again.

'Say that last bit again,' she suggested, frowning at him now.

'Which last bit?'

'The bit about being afraid you wouldn't find me, or worse—the bit after "or worse".'

He tried to think what he'd said but the words had come out in such a rush they'd disappeared beyond recall.

'I can't remember.' He was probably frowning right back at her, but over not remembering, nothing to do with her, with Alex, with the woman he loved.

'You said you were afraid I might not love you,' she reminded him, speaking sternly and adding, 'what makes you think you no longer need to be afraid of that?'

He had to smile.

'Because you're still in my arms? Because I know that when I kiss you properly in a couple of seconds, you're going to kiss me back? Because the love I feel for you is so strong it cannot possibly be one-sided? We are one, Alex, you and I, destined, some would say, to be together.'

Enough of words, his hunger was for her lips.

He bent and kissed her, *properly* this time.

Alex had told herself she wouldn't respond. But only seconds earlier she'd told herself she'd escape from his hold and that hadn't worked either. Now she tried, really tried, to hold the emotions welling up inside her in check, but as his lips moved against hers, questing and exploring, her good intentions vanished and she kissed him back.

Her lips took on a life of their own, demanding and voracious, as all the pent-up love and disappointment, the heartbreak of parting and the joy of seeing him again melded into an inferno of need, transmitting itself to him through something too volcanic and elemental to be called a kiss.

Yet that was all it was. She realised that as they broke apart, silent, breathing deeply, staring at each other. Alex's legs gave way and she sank back down onto the divan, looking up at the man who'd reappeared, like a genie, in her life.

She shook her head but the image didn't go away so she knew he was real. Actually, the taste of him on her tongue and the slight soreness of her lips told her he was real. He crossed the room, two strides, and took her only chair from beside the table, bringing it across to sit in front of her.

'If I sit on that thing you obviously use as a bed, we won't talk and we need to talk, Alex, both of us. I will start for I have wronged you in too many ways to count.'

He reached out and took her hand, holding it, as he had once before, in both of his.

Touched her palm.

'Did you keep my kiss?'

She held out her other hand, fingers curled as if holding something.

'It's safe in here,' she said, and the smile he gave her, so full of love, flooded her body with happiness.

'That is good,' he said, serious again, 'for with that kiss I gave you my heart.'

She could only stare at him, words beyond her. Did he mean it? Had he loved her back then but not asked her to stay? What—?

He held up one hand as if he sensed her questions.

'That night, in the colonnade, I came with the intention of asking you to marry me, to stay on in Al Janeen as my wife—a real wife, not just a *misyar* one. In some ways I was confused and uncertain about that because the time had been so short, yet I knew, deep inside me, I had found a very special love, a love that would not only last forever but would grow and flourish into something beyond imagining.'

Alex shook her head. Just so had she begun to feel, although she'd had no idea Azzam had shared those feelings. Should she tell him? Was it her turn to talk? This was so unbelievable, sitting here in her tiny bed-sit with a prince telling her of his love. How had Cinderella managed it?

He touched her lips, telling her he wasn't finished, and she guessed she wasn't going to enjoy whatever was coming next.

'Before I could speak to you, Clarice came to me, she told me she was carrying Bahir's child, and unless I married her, she would return to America and bring him or her up there. Later, when my mind was less confused, I realised she wanted nothing more than to stay on in Al Janeen, but as the queen she'd always believed she was, not just as Bahir's widow. If you understand families, you will understand I could not let her take Bahir's child to America, to grow up not knowing his or her heritage and people; to grow up perhaps with a stepfather with different values and beliefs, who saw no need to instil the right principles in the child.'

Alex imagined the scenario only too clearly. Hadn't Clarice told her the plane was booked to fly her, Clarice, home to the U.S., taking Bahir's unborn child with her?

'She blackmailed you?'

Azzam shook his head.

'It's an ugly word, Alex, one I doubt you even understand, but in effect that's what it was. She… required, I suppose is the word, that I marry her, even wanted it to be immediately, but I could not marry my brother's widow before the mourning period was over—the very idea was beyond consideration. But I knew I had to save the child—my brother's child—and so I agreed.'

'And now?' Alex prompted. 'What's happened now?'

'She isn't pregnant, never was,' Azzam said bitterly. 'She lied when she first told me, even showed proof with a test stick one of her women friends gave her. Later, when she was still insisting on an immediate marriage, I began to wonder and arranged for her to see an obstetrician and that's when it all came out. But in deceiving me that way, she made me hurt you. That is what angers me most, that she made me cause you pain.'

'Oh, Azzam,' Alex said softly, and she slid off the couch to kneel beside him so she could put her arms around his waist and rest her head against him, knowing words alone wouldn't heal the hurt he was feeling. 'You did what you had to do. Believe me, I know about family.'

He didn't answer for a moment then he tilted her chin so he could look into her face.

'Tell me,' he commanded, and she found herself obeying, telling him of Rob, of his job in the bank, of his need for 'stuff', as she'd always thought of it, and the embezzlement, then his stupidity in thinking he could borrow more to pay it back, her mother's shame and drawn-out death from cancer, and her—Alex's—determination to protect her brother's wife and child from the money-lender and to clear the family name.

'I'm getting there,' she said, 'and I didn't thank you for paying me those wages. I know you must have put the money into my account because the money-lender's bully hasn't been to see me.'

'Wages? You thought all I'd paid you were some piddling wages?'

He seemed angry again.

'Why would you have paid me more? Why would I have expected there to be more?'

Azzam found himself groaning again. How stupid had he been to have even thought of judging this woman by his experience with Clarice?

He stood up, lifted the woman he loved with ease then sat down on the divan with her in his lap.

'Later, you will tell me how we can repay these debts, and maybe make life easier for your sister-in-law and niece, but now I need to apologise to you because right from the beginning I let the past and my experience with Clarice when she first came to Al Janeen influence my judgement of you. Yet that first time I saw you in the rose garden I felt something for you, and afterwards, when I watched the way you helped the children at the earthquake village and held the orphans in your arms, I understood you had that rarest of gifts, a love that reached out to all humanity.'

He kissed her neck, lifting her hair and pressing his lips to the pale skin.

'That's when I fell in love, although maybe I fell a little bit in love in the rose garden when you turned on me with such fierce anger. This is a woman with iron in her soul, I thought, and was intrigued.'

'Iron in my soul?' Alex echoed, but she'd turned her head and was kissing his ear as she spoke, teeth nipping at it. 'I'm not at all sure that's a compliment.'

He moved so their lips met.

'Believe me, it is. My country needs women with iron in their souls as leaders of the community, and I—' he kissed her more firmly '—I need a woman with iron in her soul as my consort, and in my bed as well, and as mother of my children, and grandmother of my grandchildren—'

She broke away.

'The children? I didn't think! I was so surprised to see you my mind went blank. The children are all right? Did anyone find out anything about their father? Is the new oasis dug? Is the village being rebuilt?'

Azzam smiled at her.

'The children are well and happy. The baby is starting to walk around furniture, Zahid's arm is out of the cast, and Tasnim asks me every day when you are coming back. She tells me she is learning English words from Ghaada so she can talk to you. As to the rest, you must come and see for yourself. We cannot marry yet, you and I, because of the mourning period, but you will return with me and we will be together as *misyar* man and wife, then in time we will have a more formal marriage, maybe out beside the lagoon, just you and me, Samarah and Hafa as witnesses, and the children, for they, too, are special to us both.'

Had she rubbed the lamp unintentionally? Or was this real? Alex returned the kisses Azzam was pressing on her lips, but her mind was not on kisses. It was whirling, doing sums—if the million dollars was really hers, she could pay off the debt then buy a house for her sister-in-law and niece, and have plenty left over to invest for her niece's future, enough to pay for any equipment or treatment she might need. And surely she, Alex, could fly them over for a visit, take them to the blushing lagoon and out to the village, show them the desert...

'I've lost you,' Azzam said, straightening up

and looking at her with a slightly wary expression on his face.

'It's okay,' she assured him. 'I was just tying off some loose ends in my head. I'm with you now.'

And she kissed him to show that she was.

MEDICAL™

Large Print

Titles for the next six months...

August

CEDAR BLUFF'S MOST ELIGIBLE BACHELOR	Laura Iding
DOCTOR: DIAMOND IN THE ROUGH	Lucy Clark
BECOMING DR BELLINI'S BRIDE	Joanna Neil
MIDWIFE, MOTHER...ITALIAN'S WIFE	Fiona McArthur
ST PIRAN'S: DAREDEVIL, DOCTOR...DAD!	Anne Fraser
SINGLE DAD'S TRIPLE TROUBLE	Fiona Lowe

September

SUMMER SEASIDE WEDDING	Abigail Gordon
REUNITED: A MIRACLE MARRIAGE	Judy Campbell
THE MAN WITH THE LOCKED AWAY HEART	Melanie Milburne
SOCIALITE...OR NURSE IN A MILLION?	Molly Evans
ST PIRAN'S: THE BROODING HEART SURGEON	Alison Roberts
PLAYBOY DOCTOR TO DOTING DAD	Sue MacKay

October

TAMING DR TEMPEST	Meredith Webber
THE DOCTOR AND THE DEBUTANTE	Anne Fraser
THE HONOURABLE MAVERICK	Alison Roberts
THE UNSUNG HERO	Alison Roberts
ST PIRAN'S: THE FIREMAN AND NURSE LOVEDAY	Kate Hardy
FROM BROODING BOSS TO ADORING DAD	Dianne Drake

MEDICAL™

Large Print

November

December

January